A MOMENT OF MADNESS

Emily was afraid—afraid of thinking what the fate of her son, Jeremy, might be. His running away from school had been a childish prank. But what might have happened to him could be far graver.

Emily could not stand the thought of another night alone with her fears. She could not keep from bursting into sobs before the one man she did not want to see her in such a helpless state. But the Duke of Hartford at this moment seemed to have the confidence she desperately needed, and even his arrogance seemed a mark of strength.

Emily looked at him and said, "Come with me. I cannot bear to be alone tonight."

He eyed her steadily. "Are you so very sure, Emily?"

She nodded. "Hold me, Hart. Hold me."

Even as he went with her to her bedchamber, Emily knew that tomorrow she would regret this madness. Or even worse, she might not. . . .

Lady Leprechaun

by

Melinda McRae

A SIGNET BOOK

SIGNET
Published by the Penguin Group
Penguin Books USA Inc., 375 Hudson Street,
New York, New York 10014, U.S.A.
Penguin Books, Ltd, 27 Wrights Lane,
London W8 5TZ, England
Penguin Books Australia Ltd, Ringwood,
Victoria, Australia
Penguin Books Canada Ltd, 10 Alcorn Avenue,
Toronto, Ontario, Canada M4V 3B2
Penguin Books (N.Z.) Ltd, 182–190 Wairau Road
Auckland 10, New Zealand

Penguin Books, Ltd, Registered Offices:
Harmondsworth, Middlesex, England

First published by Signet, an imprint of New American Library,
a division of Penguin Books USA Inc.

First Printing, May, 1993
10 9 8 7 6 5 4 3 2 1

For my mom, Ruth Stoltz McRae

*Who still takes wonderful care
of her little girl*

1

Lincolnshire, 1819

Faint lines of displeasure creased the delicate brow of Viscountess Darrow as she glared at the encroaching weed. With great effrontery, it had established itself in the midst of a clump of her prized chamomile. A ruthless thrust of her trowel excised the interloper from its unacceptable location.

Emily stood, brushing back an errant lock of curling brown hair that had escaped her indifferently arranged chignon. Setting down the trowel, she picked up her pruning scissors and resumed her careful harvesting of the precious blossoms. Once dried, they would be eagerly purchased by the local apothecary. Lady Darrow's herbs carried a fine reputation for quality.

Finished with the chamomile, she moved on to examine the lavender border that flanked the brick walk. The tall stems fluttered slightly in the June breeze, nodding with the weight of their thick heads. Clipping one stem, she rolled the tightly curled flower buds between her fingers, sniffing the exquisite fragrance. In a short while, they would be ready for the first cutting. She made a mental note to confirm that all the drying racks were in readiness. Lavender was even more valuable than chamomile.

June was a heady time, Emily reflected, providing the first glimpses of the garden's promise. And if the early blossoms were any indication, it looked to be a good year. It boded well for both the garden and the tenant farms.

And for another year of survival.

She had bent down to pick some ripened mint leaves when Harris announced his arrival with a hesitant cough. Emily turned and eyed the butler and man of all work expectantly. "Yes?"

"There is a man here from his lordship's school, my lady," he said in an apologetic manner.

"Oh, dear, there is not trouble?"

"He did not say," Harris replied. "I have placed him in the library."

Emily nodded her approval. "Please take him tea. I shall not be delayed long."

While Harris reentered the house, Emily darted through the stillroom doors and hastened up the back stairs to her room. It would not do to appear before a representative from the school in her dirty gardening gown. She slipped out of her old dress and pulled another from the wardrobe. After splashing water on her face to cool her cheeks and dragging a brush through her dark, tangled locks, Emily glided down the main stairs to discover the nature of the visit. What manner of difficulty had Jeremy found himself in?

As she entered the library, the man from the Norfolk Academy for Boys looked decidedly ill at ease. Perhaps her uncle had neglected to make the tuition payment this term. Pasting a welcoming smile upon her face, Lady Darrow crossed the room. "I am sorry to have kept you waiting," she said. "I fear I was dallying in the garden."

"That is quite all right, Lady Darrow."

She looked at him expectantly. "You had some message about my son?"

The man glanced nervously at the door and cleared his throat. "I regret to inform you, Lady Darrow, that your son has apparently run away from school."

Emily stared at him in total disbelief. "What?"

The school's emissary shifted uneasily from one foot to another. "Mr. Elston sent me as soon as we discovered his disappearance, my lady. I came here directly."

Emily sank into a chair, struggling against panic. Jeremy! Gone! With great effort, she tried to collect her thoughts. "When did this happen? How long has he been gone?"

"We are not certain, my lady," the man said, his color rising at the cold stare his remark elicited from the viscountess. "We believe they departed in the afternoon on Tuesday."

"They?"

"There is another boy missing as well," the man explained.

Emily closed her eyes and clenched the arms of the chair. *Dear God, please let Jeremy be all right. I cannot bear to lose him too.* "Did he say anything to the other boys? Did he give any indication of where he might be going?"

The man shook his head sadly. "We had hoped, perhaps, that he had come home."

"What of the other boy?" she asked.

"A messenger has been sent to his family as well." He forced an encouraging smile. "Perhaps they went there instead."

Emily shook her head, not soothed by his words. Jeremy was gone. Vanished, if the man was to be understood correctly, with no one knowing where or why. It was such an uncharacteristic action for her son. Jeremy was a lively lad, to be sure, but he had a steadiness and maturity beyond his ten years. If anyone had asked, she would have said running away from school was the last thing he would do.

Something must have gone terribly wrong to bring him to such a pass. But what? At each visit home he had spoken in glowing words about the school, his teachers, and the other students. Now, within weeks of the term's end, he had developed such a strong aversion that he felt compelled to flee? It made no sense. It was a rash and impulsive act—totally unlike anything Jeremy had ever done.

"It is very possible he is on his way home," the man said. "A young lad would not know the quickest route to take."

As encouraging as the thought was, Emily could not believe Jeremy was coming home. The best she could hope for was that this was merely a schoolboy lark and he would be back at school in a short time. Emily intended to be there when he returned. She wanted to hear the entire story from Jeremy himself. She would go to Norfolk, and wait.

"Are you returning directly to the school?" she asked.

The man nodded.

"Then I shall accompany you," she said, standing to add emphasis to her words. She could not remain here, sick with worry. Going to Norfolk would at least give her the feeling of doing something.

"I can assure you, Lady Darrow, that Mr. Elston is doing everything he can to find your son. He concerns himself greatly with the welfare of his boys."

"If Mr. Elston was so conscientious about the care of 'his boys,' he would not have lost mine in the first place," she retorted.

The man smiled weakly.

"By what means did you travel?" she asked.

"Mail coach. I rented a gig in Lincoln."

"Good. There will be a great number of coaches there to speed us southward." Emily started for the door. "I shall be ready to leave in an hour. Harris will show you to the kitchens if you would like something to eat."

He nodded.

Mounting the steps two at a time, Emily raced to her room. Once inside that sanctuary, she sank down on the bed and pressed her fingers to her temples.

She must remain calm. There was no reason to think any misfortune had befallen Jeremy. Perhaps it was as everyone thought—he was only coming home for some unfathomable reason. But that was such a welcome idea that she could not truly believe it. Something was dreadfully, horribly wrong. She had to find her son. And the best place to start her search was in Norfolk.

She pulled the bell rope to summon Mrs. Harris and began tossing assorted items of clothing onto the bed. There was no telling how long she would be away, but speed was of the essence. There was no time to pack a trunk. A light portmanteau would have to suffice.

And if she were very, very lucky, Jeremy would have returned to school by the time she reached Norfolk. Emily could be back to Longridge in no time, after giving Jeremy a great scold for having caused her so much worry. Everything would turn out all right, she told herself over and over, as if the words would make it true.

When Mrs. Harris arrived, Emily set her to the task of packing the remaining clothes. The viscountess returned downstairs to the library, unlocking the drawer in the desk where she kept the emergency funds. At this season, with the first crop of hay yet to be cut, it was a pitifully meager store, but she had no choice but to take it. She would even go to the unpleasant step of borrowing money from her odious brother-in-law if need be. She could not afford the luxury of pride. Finding Jeremy was of the utmost importance.

London

The Duke of Hartford lazily ran his tongue across the soft pink earlobe of the voluptuous blonde lying naked beneath him. She wiggled her body in response, and he smiled with pleasure at the reaction her movements elicited.

"My, your grace," she said in a throaty whisper. "You are in a naughty mood tonight."

"When am I not?" he asked with a grin as he nuzzled at the hollow of her throat.

"I have no complaints."

A loud pounding upon the chamber door brought a growl of displeasure from the duke. "What the devil?"

The duke's companion directed a puzzled glance at the door. "What is it, Elise?"

"I am sorry, madam." An apologetic female voice sounded through the door. "There is a man here to see his grace and he says it is urgent."

"Right now, something else is more urgent," the duke retorted, returning his attention to the ripe breasts that lay just within reach of his seeking tongue.

"Your grace!" A loud, determined male voice intruded. "It is imperative that I speak to you at once. 'Tis about the young marquess."

The duke heaved himself off the bed and strode toward the door. Flinging it open, he glared at his valet. "This had best be damned important, Rogers!"

The valet, accustomed to the sight of his master's unclothed form, did not blink an eye, but the maidservant at his side gasped either in surprise or admiration at the sight.

"His lordship has disappeared from school."

"What?"

"A messenger arrived at the house. The marquess has not been seen since Tuesday."

A cold terror swept over the duke. "Kidnapped?" His lips formed the word, but his mind could not conceive of such a horror. Surely no one would dare to do such a thing.

"The headmaster did not think so. Apparently there is another student missing as well." Rogers coughed. "The feeling is, your grace, that they ran away."

"Phillip would never do such a foolish thing," the duke said between gritted teeth as he grabbed for the clothes he had so carelessly strewn about the room earlier. "He obviously has fallen under some pernicious influence." Buttoning his breeches, he directed an apologetic look at the woman in the bed. "I am sorry for the abrupt end to the evening," he said.

"I am certain all will be well, Hart," she replied. "It will no doubt turn out to be a boyish prank."

"And someone will have a blistered backside as a result," he said with irritation as he fastened his shirt. Retrieving a highly polished Hessian from where it had fallen at the bedside, he leaned down and gave his mistress a brief kiss. "I will see you when I return."

"Take care, Hart."

"Save your concern for Phillip. He will need it when I have done with him." The duke raced out of the room, still pulling his finely cut jacket of black superfine over his shoulders as he did so. Instantly forgetting the delectable armful he left behind, he turned to Rogers. "What does the headmaster think?"

"Reading between the lines of his letter, your grace, I think he is as puzzled as anyone. He expressed hope that the marquess was on his way home."

"I thought I was paying a premium tuition to have someone watch over my son," the duke grumbled as he raced down the front steps of the cozy house in Chelsea. "By God, even those fools at Eton would be hard-pressed to lose a marquess."

His traveling curricle stood waiting in the street. Hart did not relish the task of a hasty journey to Norfolk. But he could not entrust the critical task of finding his son to the man who had lost him in the first place.

The duke gave a curt nod to the groom who waited beside the curricle, noting approvingly that his best pair was in the harness. Thank the Lord his staff maintained the good sense for which he paid them. He glanced at Rogers. "Do I need to return to Grosvenor Square?"

"No, your grace. Your bag was packed while the horses were being harnessed. You have everything you need for a week, at least." Rogers handed him a small wallet. "And funds for a lengthy journey."

"Good," said the duke, accepting the man's efficiency as his due. He clambered into the light carriage, nodding to the groom to jump up beside him. He gave a shake to the reins and his finely bred horses moved away from the curb, trotting off into the dimly lit London night.

The duke wasted little time in reaching Islington. The streets were remarkably free of traffic, owing to a profusion of grand entertainments that had not yet disgorged their revelers. The rising moon provided acceptable if not ideal lighting, and the duke felt certain he could make admirable progress this night. There was no time to waste. Phillip's safety was paramount. He would reach Cambridge—or Newmarket—tonight if he had to change horses each and every half hour.

Norfolk

On the afternoon of the next day, Emily sat in the headmaster's study, trying to listen to his placating words.

"I assure you, Lady Darrow, we are doing everything possible to locate your son." The headmaster smiled at her in his most earnest fashion.

Emily was not deceived by Mr. Elston's reassuring manner. "Yet you have not found him."

"No." The man's shoulders slumped. "This is the first time in all my years as a headmaster that I have ever seen such a thing. That was one of the tenets in the founding of the school, to create an atmosphere that the boys would find amenable."

"Have you talked with any of the other students? Did Jeremy or the other lad tell anyone of their plans?"

Elston shook his head. "Not that we have yet discovered."

"Perhaps if I spoke to them . . ." She smiled disarmingly. "Despite the congenial atmosphere, you are still a figure of authority to the students. They might be more willing to talk with a mother."

"Lady Darrow, if you feel it will do any good, you are welcome to talk to each and every one of the boys."

"Thank you."

The door to Elston's office crashed open and a disheveled and dust-covered man burst into the room. Emily shrank back in alarm.

"By God, Elston, if anything happens to Phillip . . . !" The stranger glared at the headmaster. "Has there been a ransom note? Did you call the Runners?"

Elston jumped to his feet. "I do not think it a kidnapping, your grace," he said, obsequiously apologetic.

Emily stared at the new arrival. 'Your grace'? This man was a duke? He looked more like a down-on-his-luck gamester with his wind-blown blond hair and unshaven face.

Yet he must be the father of the other runaway. And if he had sped to Norfolk with the same haste as she, Emily could understand his disarray.

"What makes you think my son left of his own free will?" the duke demanded.

"The fact that another student disappeared as well leads me to think it is some sort of boyish adventure."

"Well, I had my share of boyish adventures in my youth, but running away from school was not one of them!" the duke roared. "I thought this school was designed to encourage the boys, not force them to run away. I would expect that at Eton, but not here."

He darted a brief glance at Emily and his gaze narrowed as he examined her with a calculating look. She saw the dismissal in his eyes when he turned back to Elston, and she bristled at the slight.

The duke stared stonily at the head. "I would prefer this were a private matter," he said, with a pointed nod in Emily's direction.

"Oh, it is quite all right," Elston babbled. "She is involved as well."

The duke looked at her again and Emily felt the full force of his disapproval. Those glacial blue eyes left no doubt of his opinion of her. Emily was annoyed by his unwarranted anger.

"Who are you?" he demanded.

"The mother of the other runaway," Emily answered, biting down on her irritation.

"By God, madam, I am quite certain that your brat is responsible for this. He obviously coerced my son into this wild escapade." The duke glared at her. "You will be lucky to escape prosecution after I am finished with you."

"Now, your grace," said Elston soothingly. "I am certain there is a logical explanation for all of this."

Emily sat rooted to her chair, shocked by this arrogant man's scathing denunciation. Then, drawing herself up straighter, she fixed him with an icy glare of her own. "My son," she said with utter certainty, "would never think of leaving school by himself. I fear it is *your* son who must take the blame for this reprehensible incident."

"My son?" The duke glowered at her for another moment, then turned back to Elston. "What attempts have you made to track down Phillip?"

"No one in the neighborhood has seen them," the master replied sadly. "I sent messages as far as Norwich, thinking they would have gone there, but no one at the coaching inns recalls two young lads traveling alone."

"They could be anywhere in the country by now!" the duke exclaimed.

Elston smiled in a conciliatory manner. "I think not,

your grace. It is quite likely they are on foot. In which case it will be easier to find them."

"I am calling in the Runners," the duke announced. "And while we wait for their arrival, I want to have every inch of this district combed."

"I have several men who can assist you, your grace."

The duke nodded curtly. He turned toward Emily. "Dare I ask you for a description of your son?"

"He is ten, of medium build, with brown hair and light brown eyes," she said.

The duke snorted with irritation. "That could describe half the boys in the kingdom."

"I am sorry I do not have a son with bright green hair to make your task easier," she snapped.

"So am I," he said, turning on his heel and striding out of the room.

Emily looked with sympathy at Mr. Elston. "Are all your students' parents so overbearing?"

"Fortunately, they are not." Elston replied. "But at least, with his grace's resources, we do have a much better chance of locating the boys. If you will excuse me, Lady Darrow, I need to collect my men."

Emily leaned her head against the back of the chair and closed her eyes. It all looked so hopeless. Jeremy had been gone for three days now. He could be almost anywhere. She fervently prayed that he was on his way home to Lincolnshire—for whatever unfathomable reason.

She wondered whether the arrogant duke would have any success with his search. How humiliating to be dependent on his largesse to find her son. After only that brief meeting, she knew that she did not like his imperious manner or condescending attitudes. But if Mr. Elston was correct, perhaps Jeremy had picked the right companion for this flight. A duke would certainly have unlimited funds at his disposal to finance the search. An impoverished viscountess did not.

But oh, how galling to have to rely on a man who

blamed the whole episode on Jeremy. And how typical of his kind to place all the blame on *her* son. She suspected that the duke's precious heir was a holy terror, whose every escapade was excused by his indulgent father. Men could be such fools about children! Once the boys were found, she would certainly give the man a piece of her mind for lashing out at her son in such a manner, and for not being objective about his own.

He might be a duke, but he certainly did not have the manners of a gentleman. Emily could at least comfort herself with the thought that she was always a lady.

2

The Marquess of Stratton set down the bag he carried and turned to his companion. "I'm hungry."

"You are always hungry," Viscount Darrow observed.

"I can't help it," Phillip protested. "It's all this walking. Are you certain we really need to do it this way?"

"Of course," Jeremy replied. "If we followed the roads, they'd find us before we even leave Norfolk. You don't want that, do you?"

"No," the young marquess admitted glumly. He rummaged around in the bag and pulled out a bun. "I still don't understand why we couldn't have marched down to Norwich and taken the Flyer."

"Because that is precisely what everyone will expect us to do," Jeremy explained. "We would be hauled back to school and we would never *know*." He eyed his companion with a challenging gaze. "Or are you saying that you want to go back?"

"No, no!" Phillip protested vehemently.

"Then stop complaining. You are the one who insisted we do this in the first place."

"Yes, but I never said I wanted to walk the whole way."

"This is supposed to be an adventure," Jeremy said. "Taking the Flyer would be just like traveling with your papa."

"Papa never takes the Flyer," Phillip informed him archly. "He has his own carriage."

Jeremy rolled his eyes. According to Phillip, his father had everything.

Phillip slung the bag over his shoulder again and started off across the field. "Come on," he said with resignation. "We've got to get going if we are going to get to this town."

"Do you suppose old Elston's figured we're gone yet?" Jeremy asked with a hint of apprehension.

Phillip gave him a disparaging look. "Of course he has, stupid. Someone would have been sent to check our beds after we missed breakfast yesterday."

"Do you suppose he's told your father?"

Phillip considered for a moment and then broke into a grin. "Well, if I were Elston, I certainly would not want to admit I'd lost us."

"I hope he doesn't tell Mama," said Jeremy. "I don't want her to worry."

"Mama mustn't worry about her precious little baby." Phillip snickered.

Jeremy dropped his bag and clenched his fists. "I am not a baby."

"Anyone who worries about what his mama thinks is a baby," Phillip announced with the utter confidence of a ten-year-old.

"You just say that because your mama's dead," said Jeremy.

Phillip ignored the taunt and kept walking.

"Are you sure we need to go through Newmarket?" Jeremy asked after they had walked on for a while. "Wouldn't it be faster to go straight west?"

"Of course not," Phillip replied. "Once we're far enough away from school we can catch a ride with someone. And we need to stick to the roads to do that. Besides, I want to see Papa's horses."

"What if someone recognizes you? That won't do us any good."

"They will not know me," Phillip assured him. "I haven't been to Newmarket in an age."

"Well, if you think it is safe," Jeremy said reluctantly. "I would hate to be tracked down after traveling such a short distance."

Phillip did not want to admit that he was not totally certain which way they should be going. But he knew that Newmarket was toward the west and that was good enough for him. He would worry about their next destination later.

The two reached Thetford late in the afternoon. This was their first foray into a town of any size; they had deliberately skirted all others on the second day of their journey for fear they would be discovered. But Thetford was far enough away from the Norfolk Academy that they thought themselves safe.

"First, we need to see about getting to Newmarket," Phillip announced.

"There are a lot of farm carts about," Jeremy noted. "One of them surely will be heading there."

But after speaking with several drivers they discovered, to their chagrin, that tomorrow was market day in Thetford, and there would be little traffic leaving the city until the next day.

"Well," said Jeremy with resignation, "I guess we shall have to walk some more."

"Don't be silly," snapped Phillip. "We can take the mail coach."

"It will be too expensive," Jeremy warned. "We need to save our money for food and passage."

"Piffle," declared Phillip. "We have plenty of money. And I am tired of walking." Without waiting for Jeremy's reply, he asked the first likely-looking stranger they met for the location of the nearest coaching inn. Following the man's directions, they managed to locate it after only a few roundabouts.

"I shall take care of this," Phillip announced outside the coaching office, with very much the air of authority owing to a marquess.

Jeremy forbore from arguing further and took a seat

on the bench facing the street. He looked about him with interest, but found nothing that captured his attention.

Jeremy was beginning to have doubts about the wisdom of this trip. He almost hoped Phillip wouldn't be successful in finding them a seat on the mail. Then they'd have to walk to Newmarket and he suspected Phillip wouldn't like that at all. In fact, he might dislike it so much that he'd insist they return to school.

Jeremy had no intention of backing down from the challenge first. But if Phillip was willing to concede . . .

"We're in luck," Phillip said as he stepped up to Jeremy. "With tomorrow being market day, we will likely have the whole coach to ourselves."

"We cannot leave until tomorrow?"

Phillip shook his head. "The last coach today left over an hour ago. But the ostler said he might be willing to let us stay in the stable tonight."

Jeremy nodded. "How much is it going to cost?" he asked warily.

"Not much," said Phillip. "What say we eat? I'm starving."

As this accorded with Jeremy's own wishes, he did not protest, and the two boys headed off down the dusty street in search of something good to fill their stomachs.

The Duke of Hartford spent a frustrating afternoon riding hither and yon about the Norfolk countryside. He belligerently demanded of all he met whether they had seen the two boys, and expressed his displeasure when each and every one said they had not. What could possibly have possessed Phillip to undertake such a mad start? No doubt the detrimental influence of *that woman's* son. Hart began to wonder if the Norfolk Academy was the most suitable place for Phillip.

He would have to give the matter serious consideration after he found his son.

The duke was in a foul mood when he returned to the school at dusk. Emily looked up in anticipation when the duke entered the faculty drawing room, but one glance at his face told her the search had not been fruitful. She set her stitching aside. "I fear you did not have any success."

"No," he snapped at her as he stretched out his hands toward the warming fire.

"Jeremy is a very resourceful boy," she said. "I have faith that he will come through this unscathed."

The duke whirled about, glaring at her with his ice-blue eyes. "Why is your husband not here assisting with the search?" he demanded. "Surely he would be of more use than you. I could use another man."

Emily gathered up her sewing. "My husband is dead, your grace."

"Oh, Lord," he said, grimacing at his error. "I am sorry." He looked at her more intently. "What did you say your name was?"

"I do not believe we have been properly introduced," she said briskly. "You were too busy accusing my son of having led yours astray."

He stared at her coolly for a moment. Then his rigid form bent in a bow. "Please forgive my hasty words," he said curtly. "I am Hartford."

"Viscountess Darrow."

A look of surprise replaced his arrogant mien. "Never say that you are Stephen's widow?"

She nodded.

"By God, madam, why did you not say so?" A smile broke over his angular features. "I knew your husband well. We were at Eton and Oxford together, and then in London, we . . ." His voice trailed off as he remembered just how he and Darrow had spent their time together before their respective marriages.

"I am quite aware of how Stephen spent his time before we were married," she said.

The duke's eyes raked her in puzzled appraisal. This unimposing woman was Stephen's widow? It was hard to believe. His friend had always had a discerning eye for the ladies, and Hart could not quite imagine that this dowdy mouse had captured the viscount's attention. Perhaps she had been a minor heiress of some sort. Stephen had needed to marry money. "His death was unfortunate," the duke said with a facile smile.

"Of a certainty," Emily said sarcastically. "But I suspect if he had not died in that carriage race, he would have found another foolish way to kill himself."

The duke gave a hesitant cough. "I am sorry I was unable to attend the funeral. I was laid up with a broken leg after a hunting accident, you know. I believe I sent a note, but I suspect you had so many you would not remember."

"Yes, the notes did pour in," she said. " 'We are sorry to learn about the death of your husband and would you mind paying his bills?' "

"Stephen always did have his finances in a tangle." The duke grinned in remembrance. "I am glad you were able to manage."

Emily stared at him with a lack of comprehension.

"This school demands a heavy tuition," he said, by way of explanation.

"My uncle is paying for Jeremy's schooling."

"The estate?" he asked with growing reluctance.

"If we have decent weather for the next five years and if the crop prices do not fall any further we might ... just might have enough to live on after we pay the interest on the mortgage."

"That bad?" The duke frowned. "It was rather ramshackle of Stephen to leave you in such straits."

"I share your sentiments," she said dryly. "But that was Stephen—enjoy the day and tomorrow be damned. I admit I saw nothing wrong with it at the time. What girl of twenty would? And I envy him in a way—he never had to grow up and face his responsibilities. He will be a carefree man forever."

"While you were forced to deal with the results," the duke observed. So it had not been money that drew Stephen to her—or had he spent all of hers as well? He examined her more closely.

There was nothing exceptional in her appearance. Her brown hair was neatly arranged in an austere style. The dove-gray dress she wore did nothing to enhance her looks, and it was several years out of fashion. All in all, there was nothing about her that was memorable. In fact, he doubted whether he would be able to provide a coherent description of Lady Darrow within five minutes of leaving her presence. Whatever had drawn Stephen to her?

"Why does your son attend school here?" Emily asked, deftly turning the conversation away from her situation. "Surely a duke's heir should be at Eton."

"I hated Eton," the duke said flatly. "I would not wish it on my worst enemy."

"My husband would tell me stories.... It sounded as if it was too horrible for words, except when the students were pulling pranks."

The duke grinned. "And we pulled a few ... Did he ever tell you about the Latin master?"

"Good Lord," she whispered, eying the duke with new interest. "You must be 'Ollie.' "

He shuddered. "You see now why I hated Eton, saddled with a name like that."

"Yes, 'your grace' does have a more commanding ring to it."

"Hart," he insisted, his expression growing more conciliatory. He gestured toward a chair and she nodded for him to be seated. "What do you think those two rascals are up to?"

"I do not know," she said, shaking her head. "It is

unlike Jeremy to behave in such a reckless manner. He is a serious boy."

"Are he and my son close friends?" he asked.

"You do not know?"

"I do not recall the name of every boy my son mentioned when he was home between terms. Phillip has many friends."

"It is a relief to have you take over the search," Emily said with simple honesty. "I think Mr. Elston is doing all he can, still . . ."

"I assure you, I will do everything in my power to find those two. The Runners should arrive by morning, as well as more of my men. We will find them if we have to look under every rock in the country."

"If only we knew what they were planning . . . I can only pray that they are heading to one of our homes."

"It is possible," said the duke, standing again. "I certainly hope it will turn out to be that innocent. Now, if you will excuse me, Lady Darrow, I should like to confer again with the head. I assume you are lodging at the local inn—can I give you my escort when I depart?"

"Thank you, but that will not be necessary," she replied with a faint flush of embarrassment.

"Very well then," he said. "I hope to have better news for both of us tomorrow." Bowing in farewell, he exited.

Emily stared absentmindedly at the door long after it closed behind him. So that was the Duke of Hartford. He always had the best, the most expensive of everything. He was not at all what she would have expected; his name was a byword for excess—in women, horses, and living—yet he bore no traces of obvious dissipation.

One thing was puzzling—there was little about him to explain his rumored success with the ladies. Even living retired in Norfolk, she had heard the more scandalous accounts of the duke's exploits. From the moment he returned to society after the death of his wife, it was said he had never been without female companionship of one sort or another. He was not technically handsome; his face was rather too lean and chiseled a visage for that. Despite his amiability upon learning her identity, she could not forget the blistering tirade he had delivered when they'd first met. She knew few ladies who would be attracted by such a rough manner. Stephen's tales had painted a picture of a jolly, fun-loving fellow, not a demanding, arrogant aristocrat.

Of course, he was a duke. A particularly wealthy one. Many women would be willing to tolerate all manner of outrageous behavior for such a favorable connection. Emily could almost excuse him for his sharp tongue. He would have little need to be amiable to anyone. No doubt he had encountered little opposition in his life.

Then an even worse thought struck her. The duke had likely seen no need to make a favorable impression upon her. It was a lowering reflection, but probably earned, Emily thought ruefully. She had no illusions that she could cut a dash in even the most countrified circles. She looked exactly like what she was—an inconsequential widow living on the brink of financial ruin. A class of lady she was certain the duke had little contact with.

Why could she not have met him before, when she still belonged to his world? Then he would not have dared to treat her with such arrogant condescension.

Emily sighed. Even if they had met before, it would not have mattered. Everything had changed and she was no longer the same woman. A blind man could tell the difference, and Hartford was certainly not blind.

Why, of all boys, had Jeremy picked *his* with whom to run away?

Jeremy looked about him with growing impatience. He knew he never should have allowed Phillip to go off on his own once they reached Newmarket. But Jeremy had already seen enough horses today and he had no desire to visit the duke's stables.

He let out a long sigh of relief when he saw Phillip ambling toward him across the heath. "You were certainly gone long enough," the young viscount complained when Phillip drew nearer.

"There was so much to see!" Phillip protested. "Papa's horses all look to be in fine trim. Besides, I found out that we can still catch the afternoon coach to Cambridge. That will save enormous time."

"If we spend all our money on coach fares, how are we going to have enough to pay for the boat passage?" asked Jeremy.

"Oh, we have plenty," Phillip announced blithely. "Papa sends me lots. I still have money left from Christmas."

Not for the first time, Jeremy wished he could have as much spending money as he wanted. Then he chastised himself for the ungracious thought. It was not Mama's fault that they were poor. And in a few years things would be better. She had told him so. "This has to be the last time," Jeremy warned.

"All right, all right," said Phillip. "After this, we won't take the coach again. But come on, before it leaves without us."

At a quick pace, they headed for town, arriving just in time to board the coach to Cambridge. The driver scowled at them when they asked to ride on top and pointed toward the open door. They glumly complied.

"We will have to take one more coach," Phillip told Jeremy as they climbed inside. "So we can ride on the top."

The coach was not empty, and the sight of two school-age boys traveling in such a manner brought looks of curiosity and suspicion from the other passengers.

"You look young to be traveling by yourselves," one stern-faced matron noted. "Going far, are you?"

"Oh, no, ma'am, just to Cambridge," said Jeremy before Phillip jabbed him with an elbow.

"Is someone meeting you there?"

"Oh, yes," said Phillip. "Auntie will be there, and Uncle as well."

"You two are brothers?" she asked, with a doubtful glance.

"Cousins," said Phillip with a bland smile.

The lady stared at them as if not completely convinced of their innocence, but she did not question them further. Jeremy darted anxious glances at her for the remainder of the trip, and the moment they arrived in Cambridge he pushed his companion from the carriage and dragged him down the street.

"What's the hurry?" Phillip asked.

"I don't like that lady," Jeremy said. "She looks like the type who would cause trouble if 'Auntie' was not here to meet us. Whatever did you tell her that for?"

Phillip shrugged. "You were the one who told her we were going to Cambridge."

"Which was pretty obvious since that's where the coach was headed," Jeremy said with a note of disdain.

"I'm hungry," Phillip said. "Let's find something to eat. We can sit on the banks of the Cam and pretend we are at university."

"I am not going to Cambridge," Jeremy announced. "I plan to go to Oxford, like my papa."

"My papa went to Eton and Oxford, and since he didn't send me to Eton, he probably will have me go to Cambridge instead," retorted Phillip.

They bought some fresh meat pies from a stall in the market and walked to the river, but found nothing to spark their interest. The afternoon was overcast and cold, and there was little activity on the Cam. After the exciting bustle of Newmarket, the university town seemed to be sadly flat. They ate quickly.

"We should be moving on," Phillip said, standing and dusting the crumbs off his shirt. "Where do we go next?"

"You do not know?" Jeremy asked with dismay.

"Well, west, of course," Phillip replied.

"Which way is west?"

"We will ask someone, silly," said Phillip. "Then I suppose we have to stand alongside the road until we can cadge a ride with someone."

"Shouldn't we know where we are going before we try to find a ride?" Jeremy asked. "What if they are going in the wrong direction? How will we know? We need a map."

"Then let's get one."

"Where do you propose we look for one?" Jeremy demanded.

"I don't know," Phillip replied. "Some kind of shop. A bookstore or a stationer's, perhaps."

It took a great deal of time to locate a map that would show them the route to their destination. Jeremy was not satisfied with their find, for he thought it looked far too vague in many spots, and did not show nearly enough roads. But as it was the only thing available, he reluctantly approved its purchase. It was late afternoon before they found themselves on the southwestern road leading out of town.

Traffic was light at this time of day, and it was not long before Phillip began to despair of ever finding a ride.

"We should have just taken the coach," he grumbled. "It will take us a year to reach Ireland at this rate."

"It is going to take longer than that if you keep stopping every five minutes to complain," Jeremy said.

"Well, I don't think walking down some boring old country road is very much fun," Phillip retorted. "Some adventure!"

Jeremy scowled and was preparing a blistering counterattack when a slow-moving farm cart came down the lane behind them. "Look," he said. "Here's our chance."

They both watched as the rickety cart lumbered toward them.

"Good day," Jeremy greeted the driver when the vehicle drew close.

"G'day," said the farmer.

"Are you heading down the road apiece?" Jeremy asked.

The man nodded.

"Might we have a ride?" Phillip asked, frustrated by Jeremy's dillydallying.

"Well," said the farmer, "I suppose that might be possible. What you two be needin' a ride for?"

"We need to get to Luton," said Jeremy.

"Well, I ain't going that far, but I could take you past Harston. That'll get you partway."

"That would be fine," said Phillip quickly, and he and Jeremy hopped into the back of the cart.

The farmer was little inclined to conversation, they were grateful to find, and the journey passed quickly. Even Jeremy was willing to admit that riding in a dusty farm cart was better than walking.

There was still an hour of daylight left when they passed through Harston. Shortly out of town, the farmer pulled off the main road down a small lane.

"This is as far as I goes," he said. "You'd be welcome to spend the night, seeing as how you aren't likely to get much closer to Royston this day."

Phillip opened his mouth to accept, but Jeremy cut him off. "Thank you very much, but we will keep on our way just the same."

"Suit yourself." The farmer shrugged, and when the boys had jumped out of the cart, he urged his horse forward again.

"Why did you say no?" Phillip demanded.

"Because it wasn't getting us any closer to Royston," Jeremy explained with impatience.'

"You heard what he said. We have little chance of getting another ride. We could have had a nice, warm night and a hot meal."

"Maybe," said Jeremy doubtfully. His mother had instilled in him a healthy wariness of strangers. "Come on, we can walk another mile or two before it gets dark."

Phillip complained, but followed behind. And, as luck would have it, another farm cart came lumbering along and they were able to get a ride to the outskirts of Royston after all. Crossing a field in the waning hours of daylight, they found a small shed that looked like it did not leak, and decided to bed down there for the night.

3

The first success in the duke's search came that same Sunday, near noon. One of the newly arrived Runners reported that the boys had been spotted near Watton two days previously. Hartford hastily recalled his men from the eastern portion of the county and posted them south and west. At least the news supported his opinion that the runaways were making their way to London. Which both narrowed and complicated the search. He prayed they would be found before they reached the metropolis. Two young lads could disappear easily in the bustle of the capital.

Hart looked forward to acquainting Lady Darrow with the news when he returned to the school late in the afternoon. She was deserving of some cheering words which would bring a smile to her somber countenance. Before he could ask for her, the student who met him at the door hastened him to Mr. Elston's office.

Hart nodded a greeting at Lady Darrow and looked with puzzled interest at the red-haired lad who stood rather shamefacedly in front of the head's desk.

"This young miscreant has finally admitted he knows something," Elston said in a stern voice.

Emily gave the boy an encouraging smile. "Now, I am certain that Mr.—Mayfield, is it?—did not realize how important his information was."

"What do you know?" the duke demanded.

"Last Monday, when I was checking on the *younger*

boys, I heard some arguing in the small room. It was those two."

"And what, pray tell, were they arguing about?" Mr. Elston asked.

"Leprechauns."

"Leprechauns?" The duke glowered at Elston. "What in God's name are you teaching the students here?"

Emily ignored the duke's outburst. "What else did you hear?"

"Well, Jeremy insisted that they were real, and Phillip argued that they weren't. Then Jeremy got mad and called Phillip some nasty names. Then I think they started fighting."

The duke turned his glacial stare on Emily. "What sort of brainless idiot have you raised, madam?" he demanded. "Leprechauns!"

"Ireland," she whispered, the color fading from her cheeks. "They are going to Ireland."

All eyes turned toward her.

She smiled apologetically. "Jeremy knows leprechauns live in Ireland," she said. "If they were arguing about the subject, is it not reasonable that they would go there to prove or disprove the idea?"

"I suppose he believes in fairies and brownies as well?" The duke sneered.

Emily directed a withering look at him. "Have you never read children's stories to your son, your grace?"

"That is the function of a nursery maid or tutor."

"Well, I could afford neither," she said. "And even Shakespeare has fairies and witches—do you disapprove of him also?"

He scowled at her reproof. "The Runners have met with some success," he announced. "The boys were seen near Watton several days ago."

Emily took in a sudden breath. "Were they all right?"

Hart nodded.

"Watton is toward the west, your grace," Elston pointed out. "They could be making for one of the Western ports. To obtain passage to Ireland."

The duke thought the idea ludicrous, but with his son's safety at stake, he was willing to consider every possibility. "It may be worth investigating," he said slowly, with a pointed look at Lady Darrow. "Still, I shall wait until we get another indication they are heading in that direction. I do not want to act precipitously. They could be just as easily going to London."

"And meanwhile they travel farther from us every minute," Emily said with vehemence. "They could be on a boat to Ireland before you deign to look westward for them."

"What would you have me do, Lady Darrow?" he requested. "Send a Runner to every port city in the island?"

She flushed. "Not every one, your grace. There are only a few main ports to Ireland. Would it not be worth the effort to check them?"

The duke frowned, realizing the wisdom of her words. It was the only real clue they had and he would be a fool to reject it out of hand. "All right," he conceded gracelessly. "I shall send someone to Bristol and Liverpool."

"And Holyhead," she reminded him gently.

"I doubt they wish to trek across Wales when the other two ports are more accessible."

"I think Bristol and Liverpool will do very well, your grace," Emily said, grateful he had listened to her at last.

"I am glad that we have a plan of action," said Mr. Elston with a genial smile. Then his eyes caught sight of the young man before him. "I warn you, Robert Mayfield, that I—"

Hartford realized at last why the lad looked so familiar. "Are you Knowlton's new stepson?" he cut in.

The boy nodded.

"I should have recognized you from the hair," the duke said, glancing at the boy's red mop. "I was one of your nursemaids when you broke your leg."

Robert Mayfield's face broke into a smile. "I remember now. You taught me how to play whist."

"And an apt learner you were, if I recall," said the duke with a laugh. "How is your lovely mama?"

The boy turned beet-red. "She is—uh—fine," he stammered.

In an interesting condition, no doubt, the duke thought to himself, with an inward chuckle. He would have to look up the proud father when he returned to town. "As I recall, it was my comments on this school that decided your mama on sending you here." The duke cast a pointed look at Elston. "I hope you are finding it to your liking?"

Robert nodded. "I am sorry that Phillip ran away. He is not a bad sort." He turned a guilty look at Lady Darrow. "Jer—Lord Darrow—is all right, too."

"I am glad you thought to tell us about the argument you heard," Emily said. "I am certain it will help us to find them quicker. I thank you very much, Robert Mayfield."

The boy shifted with embarrassment, and at a nod from the headmaster, he slipped out of the room.

The duke stood. "I will send messages to my men and have them look farther westward." He glanced at the widow. "Do you wish to remain here, Lady Darrow, or can I give you my escort to the inn?"

Emily concentrated her gaze on the toes of her shoes. "I am remaining here at the school, your grace. Mr. Elston has generously prepared a room for me."

"A capital idea," Hart replied, with little thought. "If those two miscreants decide to return on their own, you will be the first to know. If I have any new successes to report, I shall send word."

Not until he was in the corridor did Hart comprehend the real reason that Lady Darrow remained at the school. If her financial situation was as dire as she made it out to be, she probably could not afford to stay at the inn. The hasty journey here must have severely strained her resources. Her acceptance of Elston's hospitality came more from necessity than inclination.

Hart uttered a well-phrased oath at his old friend for leaving his wife and son in such a predicament.

But had he acted with any more responsibility himself in those days? The only difference was that he had an endless reserve of funds to draw upon. The Hartford coffers were deep and well-lined. He could have embarked on the wildest of sprees without causing any damage to his son's inheritance. That he had not was due more to circumstance than inclination.

His expression darkened at the memory of the chain of events that had circumscribed his actions. First, his marriage, and the difficult pregnancy that resulted in Phillip's birth. The subsequent death of his wife kept him out of society while he observed an official year of mourning. With most of the Continent closed to travel, there had been little to do but remain in the country. Not that he mourned Louisa's death; that release had been a rather gratifying one, particularly since she left him with a son.

Hart grinned mirthlessly. He'd had the last laugh after all. If that woman had had her way, the child would have been a girl, just to spite him. Thank God it was Phillip, saving him from the necessity of marrying again. He had no desire to repeat *that* disaster.

Still, Stephen should have been more careful once his own son had been born. Impecunious aristocrats were as common as crippled soldiers these days; young Darrow would have a tough time of it if the situation was as bad as his mother claimed.

Shrugging, Hartford dismissed his concern. It was not his problem or responsibility. He would do what he could to locate Lady Darrow's son, because that would lead him to Phillip as well. But beyond that, there was little to be done. It was not his obligation to restore the family to solvency. Lady Darrow had relatives; let them take care of her.

As Emily lay upon the narrow bed in her borrowed room, she wondered at the Duke of Hartford. He had been Stephen's closest friend at school, though they had drifted apart after university and their respective marriages. She would probably have met him eventually, if it had not been for the tragic chain of circumstances in both their lives. How ironic that they had each lost a spouse, and now their sons were missing as well.

Hartford did not at all look like the kind of man who would have smuggled a badger into the Latin master's study. He struck her as being entirely devoid of humor. Perhaps inheriting a dukedom at the advanced age of twenty or so did that to a man. Still, she thought that if Stephen were here, he would be greatly surprised at the change in his old friend.

Hartford was most certainly not the type of man to whom she wished to be indebted. Emily had fought too many pitched battles over her firm desire to maintain her independence since Stephen's death, first with her parents, then with her uncle. Grudgingly, they had tossed up their hands at her folly and allowed her to go her own way, accompanied by their grim prophecies of her ultimate failure. So far, she had managed to confound their expectations. Barely.

The duke looked to be one more person who wished to tell her what to do and how to run her life. Emily was quite willing to allow him to expend his money and manpower in search of their missing sons—there was little point in fighting him on matters where he had a clear advantage. But if he believed she would remain here when the search began in earnest, he was sadly mistaken. She was not going to sit here at the school, patiently waiting for someone to bring her news of Jeremy. If they were heading west, toward Ireland, she would follow them no matter the cost. No amount of ducal derision could keep her from the search.

And if he dismissed the idea of Ireland as foolish, she did not. She knew Jeremy. He was deadly practical. If the existence of leprechauns was called into question, the only certain way to resolve the argument was to go to their homeland and see for himself. She was only grateful he was not alone in his quest. Two boys together were safer than one alone. And a very rich and powerful duke just might be able to perform miracles.

After spending a comfortable night in their shelter, the two youngsters hastened into Royston in search of breakfast and in hopes of finding some early-morning traveler on his way westward. Since it was Sunday, however, neither possibility was forthcoming. With a resigned sigh, they ate their bread and cheese and continued their day's trek on foot.

Not until mid-afternoon did they finally obtain a ride, but the wait was well worth it, for not only did the lone traveler agree to take them as far as Hitchin, he let drop the news that there was to be a fair there on the morrow.

Phillip could hardly control his delight. The discovery of this monumental event surpassed all his expectations for the journey. Darting a quick glance at Jeremy, Philip half expected him to offer up some argument against going to the fair. But Jeremy did not utter a word of protest, and Phillip eagerly wondered exactly what marvelous things the fair would have to offer. He only regretted that they had to wait an entire night before it began.

This regret was soon appeased upon their arrival in Hitchin, where they learned that watching the setting up of a fair was nearly as exciting as the fair itself.

Phillip and Jeremy looked on with anticipation as men unrolled tents and awnings, scrambling aside when they were in the way and generally making nuisances of themselves. More than one man chased them away. But others were willing to let them watch and help with the toss of a rope or the pounding of a stake. To the boys' great disappointment, they were not allowed a glimpse of the Wild Indian, but they were mollified by the showman's warning that such an attempt would be far too dangerous. They were given a peek at the Irish Giant and allowed to actually *touch* the deadly boa constrictor. All in all, it was a most exciting evening. They even found a place among the fair-givers to sleep, and enthusiastically pronounced fair folk as perfectly respectable fellows.

By morning it was all business, and no one had time for two young boys. Phillip and Jeremy cadged a few pieces of broken gingerbread from one of the stalls and wandered around amidst the growing crowd.

"First, we need to see the Wild Indian," Phillip announced.

"I want to see the Irish Giant bend iron," Jeremy said.

"That too," Phillip agreed. "What time are they to feed the snake?"

"The man said at noon." Both boys were determined not to miss such an exciting event, even if it cost all of a tuppence. After actually touching the animal, they viewed him with a proprietary air.

"I can hardly wait," said Phillip, cramming the last of his spicy gingerbread into his mouth in imagined imitation of the upcoming feeding. "Just think, a whole rabbit!"

Jeremy, who had several pet rabbits back at home in Lincolnshire, rather wished they fed the snake something else, but not to the extent that he would miss the wondrous sight.

With jaunty steps they wandered among the caravans

and tents, following the sounds of the drums and trumpets the showmen used to attract their customers. They dutifully paid their fees and crowded their way to the front of the admiring throngs. The menacing Indian turned out to be impressive and scary, the snake ably dispatched the rabbit, and the Irish Giant showed he was, indeed, able to bend iron. They debated long and hard over seeing the pink-eyed lady, but decided instead on viewing the body of a genuine mermaid which reposed in a glass case.

"She didn't look much like a mermaid to me," Phillip said with chagrined disappointment. "She was so small. And dried out."

"They should have a live one in a tank," Jeremy agreed.

"That's what I would like to do when I am older," Phillip said. "Sail the seven seas and capture mermaids. I could make a fortune selling them to fairs."

Jeremy laughed. "No one is going to let the son of a duke do any such thing," he said. "Besides, I'd rather go to America and look for ferocious Indians."

"Viscounts can't do things like that either," Phillip said.

"Oh, no?" Jeremy demanded. "You just wait and see. I will be a famous explorer while you are sitting in the moldy old House of Lords with a big fat wig on your head."

Phillip scowled, and when Jeremy wanted to watch the Punch and Judy show, Phillip scornfully pronounced it "for little children." Instead, they watched the dancing bear.

"I'm hungry," Phillip announced when the performance was done and they were strolling through the crowd again.

"We can watch the wrestling while we eat," Jeremy said.

"Look at the size of that man," Phillip said in awed admiration as they elbowed their way to the edge of the wrestling ring. "He's even bigger than the challenger I saw at the boxing match last year."

"You've been to a boxing match?" Jeremy asked with awed admiration.

Phillip nodded. "Papa took me last year. We went all the way in the curricle."

"Was it exciting?" Jeremy was eager for a glimpse of the sport he had only read about.

"Oh, yes," said Phillip, realizing he had an appreciative audience. "The roads were so clogged with horses and carriages you could barely get near the place. All of Papa's friends were there, and I sat with them the whole time. Papa won a good deal of money on the fight, too."

Jeremy turned to watch the upcoming match, but his excitement was dimmed by the knowledge of his friend's good fortune. Wrestling was not nearly as exciting as boxing. Someday he would see a real match. If his mother did not find out.

"Let's find something else to look at," Phillip suggested after they had watched the wrestling for a while. Despite the crowd's enthusiasm, the victories of the local champion carried little excitement for him. "I want to ride on the roundabout."

There was a line of children waiting for a ride on the whirling contraption, but after seeing at what a clipping pace the ride moved, they determined to wait for their glorious turn. Mounted upon sturdy wooden horses—the carriage box was for "little babies"—the boys screamed with glee as the ride circled around and around, propelled by the hardworking boys who pushed it.

"That was capital fun," Phillip exclaimed when their heads had stopped whirling and they could stand again.

They continued their meander through the fair, stopping to purchase gilt gingerbread in the shape of an elephant. With great care they inspected all the fairings offered at the traders' carts. Phillip agonized over whether to buy a popgun or a trumpet. Jeremy lingered longingly over the array of whistles, but then shook his head a little sadly and moved on. He did not dare spend too much of his valuable funds on trivialities. He finally decided to purchase a length of pink ribbon for his mama.

"Why did you spend your money on something dumb like that?" Phillip demanded.

"It's for Mama," Jeremy replied, and carefully tucked it into his pocket.

"Isn't that sweet," Phillip taunted. "Buying a present for Mama. What a good little boy."

"Shut up," said Jeremy, turning away and walking hastily past the stalls.

"Hey, Jeremy, wait," Phillip yelled as he ran after him. "Don't be angry. I was only teasing."

Jeremy scowled at him. "Don't do it again," he said.

"Sure," Phillip agreed. "Are you hungry now? Let's eat."

Stuffed with food and sated with pleasure, they finally crept away from the center of the fair and sprawled upon the grass.

"They're going north tomorrow," Phillip said. "Let's follow. Wouldn't it be fun to do this every day?"

"We're supposed to be going to Ireland, remember?"

"Oh, well, we can do that too, eventually. But just think—maybe if we stayed with the fair we could be the ones to feed the rabbit to the snake—or hand the Irishman the iron bar."

Jeremy looked at him with disappointed eyes. "You want to give up on our journey?"

"Only for a little while." Phillip dumped his bag out onto the grass and eagerly began examining all his newly acquired treasures.

"How much money did you spend?" Jeremy asked him with growing dismay at the sight of the horde.

Phillip shrugged. "I don't know."

"Count it quick," Jeremy said anxiously. He knew to

the ha'penny how much money he still carried. Phillip's free-spending ways irritated him. They would never reach Ireland if they ran out of money.

Phillip rummaged deeper in his bag, turned out all his pockets, and emptied out his shoe. "I've still ten pounds or so," he announced with a cheerful grin.

"You had better stop spending it or you won't have enough to get us to Ireland," Jeremy cautioned. "And if we follow the fair you're bound to lose it all. We need to keep to the journey. And not spend another penney unless we really have to—like for food and things."

Phillip frowned, as this did not at all sound like jolly fun, but he was so full of gingerbread and meat pasties and lemonade he did not care.

Jeremy consulted the map. It might be best if they took a more backways route for a while, to keep Phillip from the diversions and temptations of the towns. And according to the map, there was a perfect route. It would accomplish that aim and get them closer to Ireland as well.

He turned to Phillip with a broad smile. "Want to pretend you're a Roman soldier?" he asked.

4

Emily was sitting in the faculty drawing room on Monday morning, reading to a fascinated circle of the youngest students, when Elston scurried into the room.

"The duke is returned, my lady, with news of your son," he said.

She quickly murmured her apologies to the boys and hastened to Elston's office. Hartford stood impatiently before the desk.

"They have been seen again?" she asked eagerly.

He nodded. "In Newmarket. Two days ago." He shook his head in frustration. "I must have nearly passed the rascals on the road. I am departing now and will send word when I learn anything new."

"Take me with you," she said quickly.

"Lady Darrow, I hardly think—"

"Please?" She turned her imploring hazel eyes upon him.

"I think you would do best to remain here. I will certainly let you know when I find your son."

"I will go mad if I have to sit here and wait," she protested. "It shall not take me more than a moment to get ready."

"You cannot travel with me," he said with indignation. "A lone woman . . . It is highly improper."

"I do not care if it is proper or not, I want to find my son!" Emily took a deep breath. "I am a widow, you remember, and allowed a great deal more latitude than a young unmarried lady."

The reluctance did not leave his face.

"Then tell everyone I am your sister," she suggested. "Make up whatever story you like. I must come along. We are looking for my son, too."

"It is an open carriage," he argued. "If the weather turns inclement . . ."

"I will not melt in the rain."

"This is not a pleasure jaunt," Hart said. "If we get on their trail we could be going from dawn to dusk. There won't be time to stop for you to arrange your hair or freshen your clothing."

"My hair is of little importance when compared to the safety of my son," she retorted. "I beg of you, Hartford, let me accompany you on the search."

He opened his mouth to offer a rejoinder, then closed it again. Let her be foolish if she wished. "I warn you," he said, "I will not hesitate to dump you in the middle of a country lane if you cause me any difficulties."

"I am known to be an amiable person," she said, quickly heading for the door. "I will be ready to leave in mere moments."

Hart gave Elston an embarrassed glance and shook his head in self-deprecation. Whyever had he agreed to such a mad thing? Lady Darrow would only slow down his progress with her importunate female demands. He knew the folly of traveling with women. She would find the road too dusty, or the carriage ride too rough. No doubt he would be forced to listen to her interminable complaints all the way to Newmarket.

He would have to devise some method of discouraging her. Hart did not want to have any more worries upon his head. Lady Darrow would be one more bothersome distraction when he needed to concentrate all his attention on finding Phillip.

She was such a prim thing he was mildly surprised she had even suggested she accompany him. Undoubtedly, worry over her son had clouded her thinking.

When she realized the impropriety of the situation, she would be willing to let him handle this on his own. He had never lured a woman into an indiscretion in his life and he was in no mood to start now. He would make certain that Lady Darrow had no desire to travel with him beyond Newmarket.

Emily frantically tossed her meager belongings into her bag, fearful the duke would change his mind and leave without her if she tarried. She was nearly breathless when she rejoined him in Elston's study, tucking the last wisps of hair beneath her bonnet.

Hart eyed her with a skeptical glance. "You are ready?" he asked with some surprise at the speed of her return.

She nodded.

Shaking his head again at his folly, he picked up her bag and motioned for her to follow him out to the waiting carriage.

"You have displaced my groom, you know," he told her when he assisted her into the vehicle. He pointed at the man holding the heads of the restive horses.

"Should you prefer me to ride on the perch?" she asked with an amused smile.

Hart grinned in spite of his wariness. "No, that will not be necessary, Lady Darrow. Jacobs is more accustomed to that position. It would not do to lose you off the back when we rounded a sharp turn."

"I hope you know I am a better hand than that," she said as the groom hopped upon his perch and the horses trotted off. "I was wont to drive with Stephen, you know."

"And he never pitched you out of the carriage?" Hartford laughed. "Stephen must have developed some caution after all."

"He did land us in the ditch more than once," she admitted.

"That is something I promise not to do."

They made excellent time to Thetford, stopping only once to change horses. Another change was required before Newmarket, but they reached the racing town in what Emily knew must be record time. The duke drove fast but skillfully. It was not the duke's driving that caused her agitation to increase with each mile. It was worry over Jeremy. She hoped they would find him quickly.

"Where were they seen?" Emily asked him as they neared the outskirts of Newmarket.

"Near the race courses," he replied. He deftly tooled the horses through the town, then swung the carriage down a side lane that led to the course.

"Do you own race horses?" she asked.

"Yes, and if we do not find those brats soon, I will miss the meeting at Ascot," he said with irritation.

"How inconvenient for you," she said sarcastically.

Hartford reined in the horses and fixed her with his icy blue stare. "I did not ask you to come with me, Lady Darrow. And as I told you, I have no compunctions about canceling your participation in this adventure at any time. Do not press your luck."

"I am sorry," she said meekly while she inwardly chastised the duke. How could he even think about something as unimportant as a horse race when his only son was missing?

Hartford pulled the carriage up outside an elegant brick stable block. Tossing the reins to his groom, he hopped down and stalked off, leaving Emily behind. She debated whether to follow him or remain in the carriage, deciding finally upon the latter course. It would not do to antagonize the duke further. Unfortunately, she needed him.

It seemed an interminable time to Emily before Hartford returned. He spoke a few quick words to the groom, who then vanished into the stables.

"What did you learn?" she asked eagerly.

"They passed through here on Saturday," he said as

he climbed into the carriage. "Phillip apparently visited my stables."

Emily's heart lurched painfully. "Jeremy was not with him?"

"Someone else reported that they later saw two boys, one dark, one blond, wandering around on the heath. We can only hope it was them."

"What now?"

"We shall return to town and have a light nuncheon."

Emily stared at him with disbelief. "Your son is missing and you want to eat lunch?"

"My men and the Runners are here already and they should be able to find some trace of them. My assistance, at this point, is superfluous."

Emily would much rather have pursued the search than eat, but she dared not argue. The duke would do as he pleased, despite her objections. If she wished to remain with him, she would have to ignore her inclinations. She had no doubt he would be quite willing to leave her stranded in Newmarket if she displeased him.

But the thought of Jeremy and his friend on their own chafed at her. Saturday was all of two days ago. They could be miles from here by now. She only hoped that her theory about Ireland was correct. If they had traveled continuously these past two days, the boys could easily reach Bristol or Liverpool in very little time. Only the men the duke had dispatched to those two ports would be able to stop them.

And if the boys were not heading for the ports . . . Emily refused to think about that course. England was a very large country when one was searching for two rather small boys. She prayed that someone else had seen them when they left Newmarket, so they could know in which direction the boys were traveling. And that the duke's men would find that person.

Hartford pulled up in front of a modest inn. He wore an abstracted air as he assisted her down from the carriage. "I will bespeak us lunch," he said. "Would you like me to reserve you a chamber? You can rest while my men continue to search the area."

"I am quite rested enough," she said. She did not trust him to wait for her if he developed a lead on the runways' whereabouts.

He shrugged and Emily followed him into the inn.

"This is a pleasant hostelry," she observed, when the landlord had ushered them into a private parlor. "Do you stay here when you come to Newmarket for the races?"

"I have never stayed at this inn in my life," he replied. "Good God, woman, do you think I would take you to a place where I am known? I am trying to preserve your respectability, however lightly you treat it."

"Oh," she replied. Respectability was the last thing on her mind. Jeremy's safety was paramount. Alongside that, the mere thought of damaging her reputation by traveling with a man unrelated to her paled to insignificance. The duke's concern for such mundane things shocked her. How could anything—her reputation, lunch, or the Ascot races—be more important than finding his son?

The landlady bustled into the room with a pot of steaming tea. Emily eagerly poured herself a cup, then turned to the duke. "Should you care for some, your grace?"

"I will have ale," he said.

She nodded, sipping her tea while she eyed him with a speculative glance. "Do you accept yet that they are going to Ireland?"

He shook his head. "Newmarket is very much on the way to London. For all I know they are heading to Ascot for the races, although I never knew Phillip to hold such an interest in racing. Is it a passion of your son's, Lady Darrow?"

She chuckled. "I am not even certain Jeremy is aware that formal horse races exist," she replied.

"All the more likely he might wish to see a race, then. I'll send someone down to Ascot to make certain."

Emily took another sip of tea. It was obvious that this was going to be an awkward partnership between her and the duke. Perhaps if she could draw him into conversation, she might better take his measure. But whatever could she, who had not been in society for years, find to discuss with him? All they had in common was their sons. It was as good a topic as any. "Is Phillip your only child?"

"Yes."

"Is he a good student?"

Hart eyed her quizzically. "Do you honestly care about my son's academic prowess, Lady Darrow?"

Emily drew herself up straighter. "I am only trying to make polite conversation, your grace."

"Well, don't bother," he said. He took a large swallow of ale, setting down the tankard noisily. He sighed. "I suppose you are right, Lady Darrow. We must follow the social amenities. Very well, then. How did it happen that you sent your son to the Norfolk Academy?"

"It was my uncle's suggestion," she replied. "Stephen's death threw my family into a difficult quandary. They were saddened, of course, but rather embarrassed as well. Not to the extent that they wished to relieve me of the financial situation, but enough that they felt they needed to do something. Paying for Jeremy's school is one of those gestures."

"You still live on the estate? Could you not have economized by renting it out?"

She frowned. "It is possible, I guess. But I never really considered it. It seemed the logical thing to remain at Longridge, where I could supervise the home farm and the tenants."

"Your steward should perform those functions."

Emily shook her head. "I fear that I employ few retainers, your grace."

"Surely you do not run the entire estate on your own?"

"It is not a laborious task," she said. "It is only a small estate, after all. I merely try to ensure that Jeremy will have something to inherit when he comes of age."

Hart glanced up when the landlady reentered the room, carrying their meal on a large platter. She set the food on the table and he dug into the fresh pigeon pie with appetite.

"'Tis good," he said to Lady Darrow, washing down the delectable dish with a swig of ale.

"I am not terribly hungry," she said, but dutifully took a small bite. The tea had restored her composure somewhat, but she could not shake her nagging worry over Jeremy's safety. She doubted she would have much of an appetite until he was found.

"Suit yourself," the duke said, and hastily ate the rest of his meal.

Emily took a few bites of the pie, but finished with a slice of buttered bread and a wedge of Cambridgeshire cheese. Hartford ate steadily, but without haste. Emily wanted to shake him. After their frenetic pace of the morning, she thought he would be dashing all over the town in search of the boys. Instead, he appeared content to sit and drink his ale. She felt less than useless sitting here.

"Are we not to continue the search today?" she finally asked in exasperation.

He raised an imperious brow. "I certainly plan to do so, Lady Darrow, but I feel confident you would be much more comfortable if you remained here at the inn."

"Every moment we sit they are getting further and further away from us," she protested.

"Unfortunately, there is little that we can do until we know in what direction they are traveling," he said.

"You could begin inquiries in town."

"My men are undertaking that chore. I see no need to wander about Newmarket, advertising my presence in a most outrageous manner by asking about my son."

"Well, I have no objections to advertising my presence," she said, standing. "I intend to find Jeremy."

"My men, and the Runners, are most capable, Lady Darrow," Hart said. "Let them do what they are being paid to do. Surely you must realize that you cannot wander all over Newmarket unaccompanied. You would be more likely to receive a slip on the shoulder than any information from the horsemen."

The truth of his observations only increased Emily's frustration. "I feel so useless."

"I quite agree. But it was your decision to come. I am perfectly willing to send you home via post-chaise at any time, Lady Darrow."

"I shall not go," she said flatly.

"Then, Lady Darrow, I suggest you allow me to handle matters in my own way."

Her lips straightening into a thin line of irritation, Emily took her seat again. The duke, to her annoyance, leaned back in his chair, taking a deep drink of ale.

"Your grace?" A diminutive man stuck his head through the doorway. "They took the mail to Cambridge."

The duke was on his feet in an instant. "Have the horses harnessed," he said, then turned to his companion. "I urge you, Lady Darrow, to either remain here, or return to Lincolnshire. I promise to return Jeremy to you the moment I lay my hands on him."

Emily was already reaching for her bonnet. "I am ready to go now, your grace."

He frowned and stomped out of the room, Emily at his heels.

* * *

If the trip to Newmarket had been swift, the distance to Cambridge was covered at an even more blistering pace. Emily was forced to grip the side of the curricle tightly more than once as the duke swept by a slower-moving vehicle in a blur of speed. It brought back all the exhilaration of similar journeys with her husband in those long-ago, carefree days. How she had loved those heedless drives in the country, when she and Stephen would put his latest bits of blood through their paces. There had been no worries at the end of the road then. But the reason for this journey was never far from her mind. Jeremy must be found.

A man waved them down on the outskirts of the university town and the duke swiftly reined in his horses.

"We are in luck, your grace. The driver of the mail remembers them quite clearly on Saturday—asked to ride on top. They only had tickets to Cambridge and he doesn't know what happened to them after they left the coach. Said he didn't see them hanging about the inn later."

"Damn," said the duke. He thought for a moment. "What time did the coach arrive?"

"Early afternoon."

"They must have eaten somewhere. Check the inns—no, try the food vendors. No reputable inn would serve two young boys alone." He glanced hastily at Lady Darrow. "Do you have any suggestions, ma'am, on what your son might have done?"

She shook her head. "Your suggestion sounds as good as any."

The duke glowered at her backhanded compliment. He drove through town and halted before the mail-coach inn. "I think we shall be able to prove or disprove your theory today, Lady Darrow," he said. "Did they go south to London, or west, toward the coast?"

Without waiting for her answer, he jumped down from the curricle and disappeared into the inn.

Emily determined not to remain behind this time and

scrambled down. When she entered the inn, the duke glanced her way and frowned when he saw her, but she did not retreat.

"Haven't seen two lads," the innkeeper said. "No unaccompanied boys left on any of our coaches."

"We shall take a private parlor, then," the duke said. He took Lady Darrow's arm none too gently, and pulled her along as he followed the innkeeper down the hall. They were escorted into a small parlor, and the owner went for tea and ale.

"I suppose," said Emily, when she had shaken the dust from her skirts, "that you intend to wait here at the inn until more news arrives."

"I do not," said the duke. "And neither shall you. This mad start of yours has gone on long enough. I will order up a post-chaise and send you back to Lincolnshire in comfort."

"I will do no such thing," Emily insisted. "Nor shall I remain in this inn all afternoon. I intend to look for Jeremy."

He shrugged. "I will not keep you a prisoner, Lady Darrow. If you chose to leave this inn, I will not stop you. I make no promises, however, that I shall be here when you return. If a trace of those scamps turns up, I shall be gone."

"I accept the risk," she said, remembering with what haste they had left Newmarket. It was possible she would be left behind. But she could not sit by and remain inactive any longer.

The duke nodded and dismissed her with a wave of his hand. "Do what you will."

Emily left the inn. She stopped for a moment, looking about her at the unfamiliar university town. What would Jeremy have done in Cambridge? She pressed her fingers to her temples. Think!

Nothing, however, came immediately to mind, so she began to walk down the street, glancing inquisitively into each shop window she passed. What might have caught her son's attention? The drapers, certainly, he would have passed by without a glance. The apothecary? Jeremy was rarely ill.

She completed the length of the main street, crossing at last to the other side. In a university town, there might be all manner of shops tucked into the back streets or nearer the college buildings. What would Jeremy do?

It was as she was crossing one of the narrow side streets that a sign caught her eye. "Messrs. Weldon and Fife, Booksellers, Stationers," Jeremy loved books. It was rather foolish to think he would be buying books while he was running away from school, but it was the only encouraging thing she had seen. She ducked into the shop.

The bespectacled proprietor looked up as she entered.

"Good day," she greeted him, rapidly planning her speech in her mind. "I am hoping you can help me. My son bought himself a lovely penknife on Saturday with his birthday money, and now he has gone and lost it. I am not certain where he bought it, but I was wishing to look at your collection if I could. I should like to replace it, if you have the same type. Do you recall a young lad buying one on Saturday?" Emily looked at him eagerly.

"Can't say that I do," the man replied.

"He may have been with his cousin," Emily elaborated. "They are both about ten, one blond, the other dark-haired."

"Only lads I've seen here bought a map, not a penknife," the man said as he drew out his knives. "Do any of these look familiar?"

Emily could hardly contain her excitement, but calmly examined the display. "Goodness, a map seems like a strange thing for two boys to buy. I wonder if it was my nephew. He is always planning exotic adventures." She smiled at the storekeeper. "You know how boys are."

"Didn't sound like much of an adventure to me," the man said. "More of a trip."

"They were planning a journey?"

"Well, that surely seems like what they were doing. Arguing about which route to take and that sort of thing. Thought it a bit strange, myself."

"This was Saturday, you say? What on earth could they have been up to, do you suppose? I hope they have not developed some boyish fantasy about running away."

"Can't say as to that, ma'am."

"What kind of map did you sell them?"

"I don't carry much in maps—not a very great demand for them, you see. They wanted more than just the county. Found a map of canal routes that they took a liking to."

"Canals," Emily repeated, almost to herself. "Of course!" She glanced hastily at the knives. "I do not think any of these looks like the one my son bought," she said. "Perhaps he purchased it elsewhere. Thank you so much for your help." She fled from the store.

Canals. They could travel almost anywhere on the water network—London, Liverpool, or Bristol. She scurried down the street, eager to tell the duke of her find.

To her great dismay, neither he nor his carriage was at the inn.

5

Emily frantically applied to the landlord for information, but he could tell her nothing about the duke's whereabouts. Retreating to the private parlor, she sank down onto a chair in frustration. She had actual news of her son, and the duke was not here to receive it. Had he learned something on his own and left Cambridge? Hartford might very well have abandoned her, as he had threatened, and she realized with a clutching fear that she scarcely had enough money to return home—or remain more than one night at this inn.

It would be just like that high-handed duke to abandon her without a word. He cared nothing for her concerns about Jeremy's safety. The duke blithely went his way with a callous disregard for the feelings of others—the typical attitude of those with power and money. And she had neither.

Emily jumped to her feet and paced across the room. She was torn between a desire to go back outside and talk more with the shopkeepers of the town and to remain here awaiting the duke's return—if he did return.

Reason prevailed at last and she decided to stay where she was. Surely the duke would come back—and he would want to hear her news. She would wait.

Long after the dinner hour, Hartford stomped into the parlor. He shot a cursory glance at Lady Darrow as he hastened toward the fireplace, where a roaring blaze drew him to its welcome warmth.

"Have you eaten?" he asked without turning away from the fire's heat.

"No," she replied.

He looked at her then, his face full of exasperation. "Are you a fool, then? It is long past the dinner hour." Hart crossed the room to the bell rope that would summon the landlord.

"I found a shopkeeper who saw them," Emily said quietly.

"When?" he demanded.

"Saturday. They bought a map. Of the canal system."

"And?"

"And what?"

"There are no canals in Cambridge. That tells us nothing about where they are going."

"They could easily get to Liverpool or Bristol by canal," she insisted.

"And they could as easily travel to London," he answered.

"Have you discovered any better information?" she asked with a tinge of sarcasm.

The duke frowned. "No," he said curtly. His own impatient questioning had turned up no new leads. The boys had arrived safely in Cambridge, then vanished.

The landlord appeared, bowing obsequiously to what he fully recognized was a profitable client, and promised to bring dinner as quickly as possible.

"Should you not be telling the Runners of my information?" Emily demanded after the landlord left.

"I see no reason for it," Hart replied. "I am virtually certain the boys are no longer in Cambridge. Why waste time verifying that when the men could continue to scour every road that leaves this blasted town?"

Emily sat down and glanced through the many-paned window at the darkening world outside. "Night is falling," she said. "What do you intend to do?"

The duke leaned back in his chair. "Wait."

"Do you mean to spend the night here?"

"If necessary," he said. "This place seems safe enough. I hardly think to meet any of my compatriots at a mail-coach stop. Their tastes run to more refined accommodations. We will not be recognized."

Emily flushed. His concern seemed to be more for his own reputation than hers. After all, what would the *ton* say if they found Hartford ensconced in a mere posting house with an unfashionable widow? His taste would be questioned.

Although she could think of a hundred things she would rather do, there seemed no alternative to spending the night in Cambridge. They could not press on when they did not know in which direction Jeremy and the duke's son had traveled. Emily thought her money might stretch to one more night—and that was assuming she could continue to dine on the duke's largesse—then she would have to make a decision about accompanying him further. If she knew where they were going, she could have Harris forward her some money, but that was impossible when she did not know from one hour to the next where she would be.

She glanced toward the fire and saw the duke watching her intently.

"Does my plan meet with your approval?" he asked, raising a mocking brow.

She nodded. "While I travel with you, I am at your mercy, your grace."

His smug expression infuriated her.

"The Runners will be busy all through the night," he said. "I am certain that by tomorrow we shall have some notion of where those rascals are going."

Emily flashed him a wan smile. She knew the duke was only mouthing the words to make her feel better, but in her current state of hunger and exhaustion, they did contain some comfort.

The landlord entered, accompanied by two servants,

and a lavish dinner was spread out over the table. Hartford escorted Emily to her chair.

Despite her earlier hunger, Emily found her stomach rebelling at the smell of the roasted mutton. The one meat of which she could not stand the sight. She reached instead for the platter of stewed carrots, serving herself a generous portion.

"Shall I carve you a piece?" the duke asked, gesturing at the joint.

Emily shook her head. "I do not care for mutton," she replied, carefully buttering a slice of bread.

The duke gave her an odd glance, then shrugged and returned to his meal.

Emily finished her light repast long before the duke, but she was reluctant to go to her room. Perhaps when he was done eating, the duke would be in a conversational mood. She did not wish to be alone with her fears quite yet. In many ways, they were no closer to finding Jeremy than they had been in Norfolk. These few tantalizing glimpses of his progress across England only served to fuel, rather than diminish, her worries.

"Excellent claret," the duke said as he sampled the inn's offering. "Shall I pour you a glass?"

"A small one, if you please," Emily said. She slowly sipped the red liquid, waiting for him to speak. As if he wished to confound her, he continued to sit in silence.

Perhaps he did not wish to indulge in idle conversation. It *was* a rather foolish pastime when both their sons could be in mortal danger.

Or worse yet, perhaps he had no desire to converse with *her*. It was a lowering feeling to think he regarded her as more of a nuisance than a female companion. Ladies deplored the excesses of a rake, but it was a clear insult to be denied their attentions.

But why should Hartford pay any attention to her? She had invited herself along on this journey quite against his wishes. She could not expect him to treat her like a close friend. After all, he blamed her for this whole sorry episode. He probably felt more in sympathy with the innkeeper than with her.

Hartford cleared his throat and Emily berated herself for looking at him with such expectancy.

"In the morning, Lady Darrow, there is a coach leaving for the north. I strongly urge you to take it home."

"Why?" she asked.

"Because I have no way of knowing how long this mad chase will take, nor where it will lead us," he explained. "You will be better off in the security of your own home."

"While my son wanders about the country alone, and in danger?" she asked in exasperation.

"Your insistence on traveling with me will do nothing to protect him," Hart said. "And it can only cause you harm."

"I find your excessive concern for my 'reputation' patronizing, your grace. I am a grown woman, capable of governing my own behavior." Emily drew herself up indignantly. "Since I am the one with something to lose, should it not be my choice whether to continue on this journey? Or are you one of those men who do not think women are capable of making decisions for themselves?"

The duke's features turned hard. "I would never seek to force a lady to bow to my will," he said coldly. "However foolish I thought she was."

"Good," Emily replied, setting down her glass. "I shall not return home. As I am certain you wish to make an early start, I will need my rest. Good night, your grace." She rose and swept out of the room with what she hoped was regal disdain.

Despite all her worries over Jeremy, the day's frantic travels and the softness of the inn's excellent bed combined to lure Emily into sleep. She awoke once, startled out of sleep by some strange noise, but soon drifted back into slumber.

A loud pounding upon the chamber door awakened Emily. "Be downstairs in ten minutes!" the duke commanded from the hall.

Emily sat up with a start. Judging from the light peeking through the curtains, it was morning, but she had no idea what hour. The chambermaid's light rap on the door was followed by a steaming cup of tea and water for washing. Dressing as quickly as she could, Emily hastened down the stairs.

The duke was in the parlor, wolfing down an impressive slab of ham. His eyes held an appreciative gleam when he spotted her.

"I give you credit for one thing, Lady Darrow—you are certainly able to ready yourself with haste."

"You have news of the boys?" she asked impatiently.

"Yes, they were spotted to the south of here." He gestured toward the plate of ham. "Please eat something. I do not know how long it will be before we stop again."

Emily sat down. The news filled her with a vague sense of surprise. "Then it appears they are going to London after all."

The duke took a healthy swig of ale. "Perhaps. They were seen in Royston, which is not on the main Cambridge-to-London road." He cleared his throat. "That direction would make sense if they were traveling toward Aylesbury," he said.

"What is at Aylesbury?" she asked.

"The Grand Junction Canal."

Emily's mouth dropped open. "So you do think they might travel on a canal! Will you also accept that they are making for one of the western ports and Ireland?"

He shook his head. "The Grand Junction leads to London, Lady Darrow."

"Are your men on the way to Aylesbury?" she asked.

He nodded. "Those brats are still several days ahead of us, but the Runners should be talking to the canal men by this afternoon."

"Are we going to Aylesbury as well?" she asked.

"Not yet," he replied. "I do not want to get ahead of them in case they are up to some other mischief. But we are going to Royston. Hopefully, we shall find more information there." He stood and stretched. "Are you ready to leave?"

"I shall need to pay the landlord," she said, grabbing up her reticule.

"I have taken care of it," said the duke, heading for the door.

"I cannot allow you—"

"I see no point in wasting time straightening the matter out now when we could be on the road," he said reproachfully. "If you like, I shall give you a full accounting later."

Emily nodded and followed him outside to the curricle. The duke's generosity only inflamed her embarrassment over her sad lack of funds. But at least she would not be reduced to begging at the side of the road for enough money to return home when all was done. She could only pray that the boys would be found before her expenses mounted to an astronomical amount. She must repay him.

The duke finished helping Lady Darrow into the carriage and was walking behind to climb into the driving seat when he heard himself hailed.

"Hartford! What the deuce are you doing here?"

Hart groaned at the sight of Alderley. Why, of all the people he knew, did it have to be him—the biggest gossip of his acquaintance? "I shall handle this," he said in a low undertone to Lady Darrow.

Leaving the horse in the hands of the hostler, Hart

stepped into the street. At least this way Alderley would not get a close look at his companion. But Alderley was too fast for him, tossing his reins to his tiger and hastening forward to meet Hart.

"Lost your way?" Alderley teased.

"I could ask the same of you," Hart said in greeting. "London growing too close for you already?"

"Rum luck at White's. Run off at the legs," Alderley replied. "Needed a quick trip home to replenish the coffers before Ascot." He directed a warm smile at Emily, his eyes lit with curiosity.

"A relative," Hart explained.

"Didn't know you had any family near here," Alderley responded with a sly wink.

"Distant connection," Hart said glibly.

Alderley doffed his hat with a flourish. "It is a pleasure to meet a relative of his grace," he said, his eyes raking Emily in a frank perusal.

She colored at his attention.

"Must be a pretty important connection to have you here with Ascot starting up," Alderley said with a pointed look at Hartford. "You must be confident that your horses will run well, as usual."

"A few minor legal matters that need settling." Hart cast Lady Darrow a paternal glance. "You know how the ladies are. Need a man's hand to set things right."

"A rather enchanting relative," Alderley murmured, his eyes narrowing as he perused Emily more carefully. "Dare I ask for an introduction?"

"No," Hart said firmly. "And we are late to the meeting with her solicitor. So, if you will excuse us . . ."

Alderley smiled knowingly at the duke's excuse. "Perhaps some other time . . ." He directed another look of frank admiration at Emily before he darted back across the street.

"Damn," said Hart as he climbed into his carriage.

"Someone you did not want to see?" Emily asked.

"Someone I particularly did not wish to see," Hart said. "Alderley is the biggest gossip in London. Town will be buzzing with the news within days, I can be certain."

"Particularly when you acted so secretive about the whole matter," she said. "Refusing to introduce me was a sure sign you had something to hide."

"What was I supposed to do?" Hart demanded. "Tell him I'm jauntering about England with the widow of Viscount Darrow?"

"If you had given him a name he might have believed that bouncer about a legal matter." Emily glared at him. " 'Need a man's hand to set things right.' I am perfectly capable of taking care of my own legal affairs, thank you."

"I am certain you are, Lady Darrow, but it seemed the easiest thing to say at the time. Should we encounter another acquaintance I will explain that you are coming along to assist me in some legal dealings. *That* will surely make a better story."

"I fail to see why the whole thing is of such concern to you," she said. "It is not as if anyone would recognize me. I have not been to town since Stephen died. Your ridiculous taradiddle will only arouse his curiosity."

"As we are leaving Cambridge within the minute, it will not matter anymore," the duke said, angered by her ungrateful reaction to his chivalry. "I promise, Lady Darrow, to make full introductions if we encounter another person known to me. Will that serve to satisfy you?"

"Yes," she said between gritted teeth. His overprotectiveness angered her nearly as much as his overbearing manner. What right did he have to take care of her? He was not her relative—or even her friend.

The weather, which had alternated the previous day between late-spring sunshine and cooling clouds, was gray and menacing today. In fact, Emily noted, with an anxious glance at the sky, it looked very like to rain. She recalled the duke's warning about the open carriage and she lifted her chin with a determined air. She had survived more pressing problems than a bit of rain in these last years.

Her determination was not quite so strong when the sudden shower hit them only a mile out of Cambridge. She drew her traveling cape closer, thankful that her bonnet was too well used to suffer much damage in the wet. In the old days, before Stephen's death, she would have been wearing a delicate, flowered creation that wilted at the merest drop of rain. He would have gleefully replaced it the next day. Now, well-woven chipstraw proved more hardy.

Hart drove with a steady hand at the reins, ignoring the elements. Emily felt a twinge of pity for him, for the hatless duke looked to be even wetter than she. But judging from the determined look on his face, he was not going to let the rain get in his way. He was as intent on finding his son as she was Jeremy.

As they neared Royston, the number of vehicles on the road increased and they were forced to slow to a pace that only seemed to emphasize the dampness around them. Despite the rain's slackening into a misty drizzle, the temperature cooled and Emily wondered just how long it would take to freeze in an open carriage. Even the knowledge that her hat would survive this drenching was losing its power to pluck up her spirits when the duke finally tooled the curricle into the main street of Royston and halted before a modest inn.

"I fear this is the best I can do today," he said with an apologetic smile. "It shall be dry, at least." Tossing the reins to the hostler, the duke stepped down and surprised Emily to the tips of her boots when he turned and helped her from the carriage. It was an unexpected act of gallantry.

* * *

While escorting Lady Darrow into the inn, Hart could not help but be impressed with her aplomb. She had endured one of the most miserable carriage drives of his life without a word of complaint, even though he knew she must be wet and freezing. He certainly was. He began to think that under Lady Darrow's unprepossessing appearance lay a woman of steel. Her determination to accompany him on this mad chase certainly indicated she was made of sterner stuff than most. All his efforts to discourage her from continuing on the journey had gone for naught. Trust Darrow's widow not to be put off by a bit of fast driving and wretched weather.

He quickly garnered them a small private parlor and noted with welcome relief that a fire blazed cheerily in the grate. Hart slipped out of his wet driving coat and draped the garment over the back of a chair to dry.

The duke told Lady Darrow to change out of her wet clothes, and the innkeeper escorted her to a room. Hart gratefully accepted the glass of hot punch the innkeeper returned to offer him moments later. He settled into a chair near to the fire and prepared to wait for either Lady Darrow's return or the advent of news from one of the Runners.

When the tale of leprechauns and Ireland was first presented to him, Hart had dismissed it as nonsense. Phillip had more sense than to become involved in an argument about imaginary creatures. But each new discovery of the boys' progress did nothing to refute Lady Darrow's theory that Phillip and Jeremy were traveling to Ireland. Hart had the rather disconcerting feeling that he would be thoroughly vexed if her guess proved correct.

Her unwavering tenacity disturbed him, whether it be her conviction that Ireland was the boys' destination or her refusal to consider the ramifications of their traveling together. He did not like independent, headstrong ladies. Had she been any other woman, he would gladly have abandoned her in Cambridge without a moment's thought. But because she was Stephen's widow, he felt he owed her something for his old friend's sake. If they were very careful, no one would ever learn of this scandalous escapade. He did not care a fig for himself, but the impoverished widow of a viscount could not afford such a cavalier attitude. It was his duty to see that she would not suffer any harm. One of them had to maintain a clear head throughout all of this.

He had struggled against the urge to plant Alderley a facer back in Cambridge for looking at her in that leering way of his. Had he not been able to see she was a lady? And a properly escorted one at that. She did not deserve such ungentlemanly glances. Of course, Alderley would leer at anything in a skirt.

Hart was forced to admit that Lady Darrow did have a certain attractiveness about her. No one would call her a beauty, but there was something about her composed demeanor that drew a man's attention. There was intelligence in her soft, hazel-brown eyes, and the hint of a sense of the absurd that he suspected would be more pronounced if she was not so worried about her son.

More important, she endured hardship like a trooper. She had not uttered one word of complaint—not only about the rain but about the discomforts of traveling. He could not think of a single lady of his acquaintance of whom he could say the same. Lord, his wife had driven him mad in less than a day on that head. Lady Darrow was a very unusual woman.

Was that what Stephen had seen in her? Had he sensed that she would be more than an ornamental wife, would also be a companion to share fun and adventure? Although Hart really wished that Lady Darrow would take his advice and return home, he had to admit that her presence was not as burdensome as he had anticipated.

If she continued to be so amiable, he would allow her to continue on the journey. But at the first sign of trouble, she would be left unceremoniously behind. He would not risk Phillip's safety for anyone.

Emily passed a desultory afternoon at the inn. The duke went out after midday, but she was content to remain behind. If he had not left her in Cambridge, she rather thought he would not abandon her here either. The innkeeper found her a book and she appreciated the opportunity to remain warm by the fire. Hartford promised to come back for her if he learned anything of note.

When the duke returned at dinnertime, wet, cold, and tired, his discouragement spoke for itself. It did not take a great deal of perspicacity to know that he was not in the mood for idle chitchat this evening, so Emily uttered no more than a pleasant greeting while they awaited supper.

That meal, however, managed to spark the duke's interest. Or at least the serving of it did. Emily frowned at the manner in which the duke admired the buxom barmaid who brought their food. The woman was well aware of his interest, and ignored no opportunity to display her charms while she set the dishes on the table. Emily suspected Hartford might have demonstrated a less-silent admiration if she had not been in the room.

Even in Lincolnshire, Emily was aware of the duke's great reputation as a womanizer. Stephen himself had told her stories of their escapades together before marriage. As a widower, Hartford had behaved with equal abandon.

Yet she thought the duke would be little interested in a country barmaid. After all, was he not accustomed to the most elegant of women?

Emily glanced up, noting Hartford's smirking grin as the barmaid leaned against him, brushing her breasts across his arm as she lay his plate before the duke. He enjoyed every minute of it, Emily thought with unconcealed disdain. Apparently he only abhorred gently bred women from the country. The memory of his disdainful glance at their first meeting still rankled.

She had no desire to sit back and cool her heels in some out-of-the-way inn while the duke indulged his sensual appetites. So far, his single-mindedness in the pursuit of his son had impressed her. But it looked now as if he were willing to become distracted. That she could not allow.

Emily cleared her throat. "Do you still believe the boys are headed to London, your grace?"

The duke looked up, amusement bright in his light blue eyes. "It seems the most likely course. I suspect we will find some trace of them on the Grand Junction," he said. "Unless they traveled directly south from here."

"Should we not have heard something by now?"

He shrugged. "We receive word of them by pure chance," he said, then smiled ruefully. "Despite my ardent desire, the entire population of England does not seem to be on the lookout for two young boys."

The parlor door opened. Expecting the landlord, Hart looked with surprise at the man who stood there, his sodden clothes leaving pools of water upon the floor.

"There was a fair in Hitchin two days ago, your grace," he said with a long outrush of air. "I've got men tracking down the caravans now. Methinks the boys might be with them."

6

The duke was on his feet in an instant, dinner and the barmaid quickly forgotten. "Tell me everything you've learned."

Emily leaned forward, praying this was the clue they needed to find Jeremy at last. "The boys were at the fair?"

The man shook his head. "I cannot say that they were for certain, my lady. But with the town so crowded, two lads would be easy to miss."

"So we do not actually know they were in Hitchin," the duke observed, sinking back into his chair.

"No, your grace. But being that they were in the area the day afore, it's likely they knew of the thing. Can you imagine two lads missing a country fair?"

"Not at all," agreed the duke. He looked at Emily. "Do you wish to proceed to Hitchin, or shall we remain here this night?" He glanced about the modest room with a faint smile. "This is not exactly an elegant accommodation, but it is clean," he observed. "And dry."

Emily's immediate reaction was to race to Hitchin as fast as they could. But the fair had been two days ago. The boys would not be there, either. Best to rest tonight and get an early start in the morning. "I am agreeable to that," Emily said. Spending the night here might prove less expensive than another accommodation, as well.

"Good work, Roberts," the duke said, dismissing the

messenger with a wave of his hand. He resumed his seat, and his dinner.

In contrast to yesterday's exhaustion, Emily did not feel tired when she lay down upon her bed. She tried to convince herself they were making progress in finding Jeremy, but she could not avoid the fact that they were still days behind him. So much could have happened in that space of time.

She pulled the covers closer against the chilly night. She wondered if the duke was sleeping any better than she. Perhaps he was not sleeping at all, she thought with a twinge of irritation. Although the barmaid was certainly not in the same class as his usual women, Emily had no doubt that what she offered was the same. Was the duke now enjoying the girl's favors in his bed, frolicking naked between the sheets?

Emily's cheeks burned crimson at her shocking thoughts. What did it matter to her what the duke did in his bed? He was free to lead the type of life he wished. He certainly did not need a country widow's approval.

Yet the very thought of the duke's amorous exploits caused a wave of longing to rush over her. She had resigned herself long ago to remaining a widow. There were no eligible men in her neighborhood, and what man in his right mind would wish to wed a poor widow and take on her son as well? Not many. And none she knew.

Over the years, Emily had grown accustomed to the loneliness; in fact, she was usually too busy to think of it. But it crept up on her at times like this, her deep need to be held and comforted by another. No manner of hard work, or love for her son, could ever quite erase the loneliness. The thought that Hartford was sharing his bed with another, however temporarily, intensified her longings. If only Stephen were still here . . .

Emily forced her dispiriting thoughts away and firmly refocused her mind on Jeremy. When she found him, she would not know whether to take him up in her arms or thrash him. He could have no idea what this wild escapade was doing to her. She had tried, over the years, not to cling to him too closely, but she knew that she still protected him overmuch. However would he make his way safely across the width of England with only another boy at his side? A thousand calamities could befall them, and the most terrifying thought was that she might never know.

She brushed back the tears that sprang to her eyes. Trust her to become morose in some tiny country inn, where there were no pressing household duties or gardening chores to take her mind off things. All she could do was stare into the dark and worry. And she had endured far too much worry over the last eight years. Was it never to end?

In his room, the Duke of Hartford slept soundly. Alone.

"I don't know why you insisted we take this way," Phillip grumbled as he plodded along the wooded path. "Being a Roman soldier is boring. There's nothing interesting to see."

"Better nothing to see than to be bothered again like we were in Luton," Jeremy reminded him. "The only people we are likely to meet here are other walkers like ourselves."

"I still don't know why you were so worried about that man back there," Phillip continued. "He was willing to give us a ride and lunch as well. He looked to be a swell."

"All the more reason not to accept the offer," Jeremy retorted. "What would he want with the likes of us? He was up to no good."

Phillip shrugged his partner's apprehensions aside. "How much further do we have to follow this stupid old road? I bet no Roman soldier ever walked down it."

"It is not much further," Jeremy said. "We will have to join the main road again if we intend to get to Abingdon."

"Where are we now?" Phillip demanded in a plaintive voice.

Jeremy squinted at the sun. "Probably due east of Oxford."

"Oh, good, I want to see Oxford."

"We are not going to Oxford," Jeremy reminded him. "We need to veer south to meet the canal."

"But I want to see Oxford," Phillip protested.

"Why? You said yourself your papa was going to send you to Cambridge."

"I want to see it," Phillip persisted with a stubborn air. "I am tired of walking on this old, boring path. I want to stop in a town and get something decent to eat again."

Jeremy thought. Oxford was not so very far out of their way. But who knew what next might catch Phillip's attention after that? Better to stay with their plan. "No," he said. "It will be just as dull as Cambridge. We need to get to the canal."

Phillip halted, dropping his bag to the ground. "I want to go to Oxford and I am going to go there," he announced with all the imperiousness of a future duke.

"Well, I'm not," said Jeremy.

Phillip glared at him. "We have been doing what you wanted this whole trip," he complained.

"Whose idea was it to ride on the mail?" Jeremy pointed out.

"Yes, but it was your idea to take this stupid Roman road," Phillip said. "And it's boring."

"You were the one who wanted to watch cheese being made," Jeremy said. "Talk about boring . . . You are just afraid to continue on this trip."

"Am not."

"Are so."

"Am not!" Phillip leaped forward and pushed Jeremy to the ground.

Jeremy got quickly to his feet. He lunged at Phillip and both fell to the ground, rolling in the dirt, kicking and scrambling. Phillip grabbed at Jeremy's shirt, ripping it down the front. Jeremy retaliated in a like manner. Then Phillip's elbow caught him in the nose. Blood dripped from the damaged appendage, but Jeremy did not waver in his determination to force Phillip to admit his cowardice.

"Say it," he said, after finally gaining the advantage. He held Phillip firmly to the ground by the device of sitting on top of him. "Say it."

"No," said Phillip, whose face was more streaked with blood than the injured Jeremy's. His arms flailed at his attacker.

Jeremy grabbed one wildly waving arm and tucked it under his knee. The other wrist he clasped with his hand. "Say it!"

"I'm not afraid to go on," Phillip gasped. "I just want to see Oxford, you dummy. We haven't seen anything interesting for days!"

Jeremy eyed him warily.

"Besides," Phillip continued eagerly, "the sooner we get to Ireland, the sooner we will have to go back to school. We could be gone to end of term—all summer even—if we drag the journey out."

"We daren't run out of money," Jeremy said, relaxing his hold on his prisoner.

"We shan't," Phillip assured him. "We won't take the coach again, I promise."

"Well . . ." Jeremy said, a reluctant expression on his face. He took a long look at Phillip and laughed. "You certainly don't look like a marquess now!" he chortled.

Pushing his tormentor off, Phillip sat up. "Your nose is bleeding," he charged.

"Yeah, but it bled all over you," Jeremy said, still laughing.

Phillip looked down at his shirt, streaked with Jeremy's blood. "Ugh." Then he laughed as well.

"My mama would have a fit if she saw me like this," Jeremy said, and laughed even harder.

"She probably wouldn't even recognize you," Phillip said.

"Well, it's certain that your father would not recognize you. You look like a London street sweeper!"

"You look like a farm boy," Phillip rejoined. "A really dirty farm boy. A pig-keeper! That's it. Lord Pig-keeper!" He collapsed in giggles.

Jeremy looked down ruefully at his dirty and torn shirt. "My shirt is ruined," he said. His mother would be furious.

Phillip shrugged. "You can buy another. They probably have lots of shirts in Oxford."

Jeremy clambered to his feet. "Then we better start walking," he said. "Oxford's still a ways away."

Phillip stood and picked up his bag, a big grin brightening his face. "Lead on, Lord Pig-keeper."

It took only a short time for Hart and Emily to reach Hitchin in the morning. He surveyed the trampled grass that marked the site of the Hitchin fair. It gave him comfort to know that Phillip *had* been here. The Runners had finally tracked down the traveling caravans and verified that those two young rascals had been hanging about while they set up in Hitchin, and spent most of the following day at the fair.

Hart was surprised to find that the boys had not joined the caravans. Had he not once thought it would be a marvelous life to be part of a traveling fair? Childhood memories tumbled through his brain. He could almost smell the tang of freshly baked gingerbread and hear the raucous cries of the showmen as they lured eager crowds to the amazing sights. How long had it been since he had attended a simple country fair?

Of course, Hart thought with a wry grin, he had been about Phillip's age at the time he wanted to run off with the caravans. Now, the life of a traveling showman did not look nearly as appealing. He was quite content to be a duke. But he was still astounded that the two lads had shown more forbearance than he would have at that age. What mission were they on that even the lure of a fair could not draw them away?

Was it as Lady Darrow thought, that they were really making their way to Ireland? It was beginning to look more and more like it, but he could not shake the nagging doubt that his son would ever do anything so foolish as worry about the existence of a bunch of Irish fairies. They could still be making for the Grand Junction Canal, and London. The delights of the metropolis might be the one thing that would draw such rambunctious lads away from a traveling fair. There was no end to the mischief they could make in the city.

As well as the trouble they could pitch themselves into. Every time he thought about the dangers that threatened his son, Hartford cringed. Ten-year-old boys had no business traipsing about England on their own. He only prayed they could be caught before disaster befell them. He knew he would not forgive himself if anything happened to Phillip—and he suspected Lady Darrow would hold him equally to blame for her son's fate.

But damn it, it was not his fault that they had gone off on this wild start. She had to accept at least equal responsibility for that. After all, her son was as involved as his. There was no telling which one of those brats had conceived this ill-considered escapade, but if it actually had anything at all to do with leprechauns, the finger of blame had to point squarely at Lady Darrow.

He turned and looked at the lady in his thoughts. She

was surveying the empty field, a wistful smile on her face.

"I am sorry we arrived too late," she said. "It has been a long time since I was at a fair." Her expression grew thoughtful. "I remember Stephen and I attended one, right after we were married. We stuffed ourselves with food and he bought me all sorts of cheap, tawdry trinkets." A faint smile touched her lips. "It was enjoyable."

"We should get back in the carriage," Hart said, taking her gently by the arm. "The men will bring word to us at the inn when they learn anything new."

"Should we not continue westward?" she asked as he handed her into the curricle. "We know the boys are not in Hitchin."

"I do not wish to advertise my presence in Stevenage or Luton," the duke said. "The roads there are too well traveled. Hitchin will do for the present."

Perhaps he thought there would be more willing barmaids in the smaller inns, Emily thought primly to herself while she settled her skirts around her. Once again she wondered exactly how—and with whom—the duke had spent the previous night. But Emily could not argue with his desire to remain inconspicuous. She would also owe him less money while they stayed at the modest hostelries. And that became ever more important as their search dragged on. She did not wish the mortification of having to tell him she could not repay her expenses until after the harvest. She still had her pride, if little else. And she did not want to be indebted to him, of all people.

Hart looked with undisguised dismay at the greasy stew in the bowl before him. He then looked up at Lady Darrow, who viewed her meal with equal distaste. "This is not acceptable," he said with studied calmness to the serving girl at the Hitchin inn.

"It's what we be serving today," she said.

"It will not do," Hart repeated coldly. "Perhaps you should send the innkeeper to speak with me." He nodded at the bowls. "You can take those with you, as well."

Emily looked at him with discountenance. "It is not that bad—"

"Yes, it is, and I will not tolerate it."

The nervous serving girl hastened into the hall. Hart's temper grew as he waited for the innkeeper to appear.

"Wot's the problem?" A short, rotund man, reeking of ale, bounced into the room.

"Nothing," Hart snapped. "We were just leaving."

"You can't be leavin'," the man protested. "You've got food coming."

"No," said the duke, "we certainly do not have 'food' coming. Pig slop, perhaps. But food, no."

"Well, aren't we Mr. High-and-Mighty," the innkeeper said. "Who be you to turn up your nose at my food? We serve good meals here."

"Perhaps your usual clientele is less discriminating," the duke said. "As for me, I beg to tell you there are ale houses in St. Giles that serve more palatable swill than this."

"You ordered a meal, you got to pay for it," the man said.

Hartford stood and fixed the man with a ducal glare. "My good man, consider yourself lucky that I am not going to the magistrate to fill a charge of poisoning against you." He reached into his pocket and flipped the man a coin. "'Tis more than you deserve." He stomped out of the room, not stopping to see if Lady Darrow followed him.

The sad condition of the stable offered further proof that this was a dismal excuse for a hostelry. Hart could not escape from here fast enough. He paced impatiently while the hostler hastily reharnessed the curricle.

Damn this journey and damn the circumstances that kept him on it. And yes, by God, damn Phillip for his foolish actions. When he finally put his hands on that scamp . . . Hart's fingers curled in anticipation.

He sensed movement at his side and turned to see Lady Darrow standing there, a frown of disapproval upon her face.

"Are you always so demanding?" she asked.

"I expect to be treated with the courtesy due a paying customer," he said.

"You could have reacted in a more polite manner."

The duke glared at her, his blue eyes hard. "I do not need you, or anyone else, to tell me how to conduct myself."

His remarks brought a flush of embarrassment to her cheeks and he regretted his harsh words. His expression softened. "One thing I learned long ago, Lady Darrow, is that people will only take advantage of those who allow it. I make it a practice not to." He held out his hand to help her into the waiting carriage.

They drove out of town in silence.

Emily waited until she thought the duke's anger had cooled before she ventured to ascertain his plans. She was inordinately pleased that there had been no discussion of her returning home since they left Cambridge. "Do you intend to stop at Stevenage now?" she asked.

He shook his head. "It is best to continue westward," he said. "We may as well go as far as the Grand Junction and see if the boys have been seen nearby."

Emily sat back, satisfied with his decision. His back was still rigid; the hands clenching the reins were stiff. Did he always make such a fuss over what had been a very minor matter? She darted a cautious glance at him. She had always been able to tease Stephen out of the sullens. Would the duke respond as well? A faint smile flitted over her face. It was worth a try. "The meal was not all that bad," Emily said in a chastising tone.

"Lady Darrow, it was abominable," he thundered, then noticed her teasing expression.

"Quite so," she said, her eyes glistening with suppressed amusement. "Deplorable, in fact."

"Detestable."

"Despicable," she rejoined, then broke into laughter. The duke joined in.

"The damnable thing," he said, between gasps of air, "is that I was truly hungry. I hope there is some acceptable inn between here and Luton. Without some sustenance, I fear I may become too weak to drive."

"I may be able to manage in your stead," Emily said.

Hartford glanced at her with an assessing look. Married to a whipster like Darrow, she very likely was a capable hand at the ribbons. "Would you care to try?" he asked.

"Oh, yes," she said, not bothering to contain her enthusiasm. She could not even remember the last time she had driven a team. After Stephen's death, of course, all the horses had been sold. Now there was only the gentle slug who pulled the gig. It would be a treat to drive a pair again.

Hart halted the team and transferred the reins to Lady Darrow. He watched approvingly as she adjusted the reins, testing the horses' responses. Sitting back, he folded his arms across his chest in a posture of relaxation, but all his senses were alert and he was ready to take action should she experience any trouble or evidence a lack of skill. But his theory had been correct—she was competent driver. Her hands were steady and smooth on the reins. These horses were nothing like the high-strung bloods he owned, but they were not slugs, either. Decent horses and a decent driver.

"Stephen taught you, I suppose," he said.

"My father, actually," Emily replied. "I believe it

was one of my major attractions for Stephen—he did not have to take on the task himself."

"I highly doubt it was only your skill at the reins that drew him to you," Hart replied.

Emily glanced at him. "Oh?"

"Come now, Lady Darrow, you cannot be unaware of your physical charms," said the duke, who grew more aware of them himself as each day passed. "They are certainly a match for your driving skills." He was disconcerted by the peal of laughter that greeted his awkward compliment.

"I rather thought I was driving better than *that*," Emily said. "I do not need a mirror to tell me I am no beauty."

"You do yourself a disservice, Lady Darrow," Hart said gallantly. "You have a pleasing countenance."

"I am beginning to see why you have such a reputation if you are so free with your compliments," Emily said with a quick smile. "After all this frantic traveling, even I know that I do not look my best."

"Then your best must be very nice, indeed," said Hart.

Emily did not reply. She could not believe that he was flirting with her—this must be his way of making amiable conversation. He probably knew no other way to converse with a woman. "Do go on," she urged. "Will you not now tell me my lips are like rosebuds, or my brows like the wings of an angel?"

The duke snorted his derision. "Do not tell me Stephen filled your ears with such drivel."

"Not at all," Emily said. "Although he did admire my taste in hats."

Hart directed a skeptical glance at her worn bonnet. "Let us hope that is not one which he admired."

Emily laughed. "Hardly. I assure you, my hats were much more stylish when I was in town."

"A pity you are not still in town."

She glanced at the duke. "What was your wife like?

Did you sweep her off her feet at the first ball of the Season?"

"It was a family understanding," he said curtly, leaving no doubt that it was not a topic he wished to discuss.

Emily winced. She had not thought the duke would be sensitive on the topic of his late wife—after all, he had been widowed longer than she. He must have loved her very much to still be reticent on the subject. Lord knows, she had loved Stephen with all her heart, but the years of genteel poverty his death had consigned her to had dimmed both her grief and love to a fading memory.

Would she feel her loss more strongly if Stephen's death had not pitched her into such a predicament? For when the first pangs of grief faded, anger replaced them, anger that he had died so young, leaving her and Jeremy virtually impoverished. Over the years, she had been able to look back at Stephen's character with growing objectivity, and realized that he had not been a sensible man, nor a prudent one. Had he lived, would their marriage have remained strong? Or would she have seen his flaws eventually?

Handsome, carefree Stephen, who would be twenty-four forever. Never to see where his heedless ways led, never to know that one eventually had to pay the piper. Would he have changed too, with the burden of debt and a growing family? Would he have become more responsible?

Emily shook her head. It did not matter. Stephen would never have the chance, and she could not condemn him with the wisdom earned over the years.

As they neared the next village, Hart reached over and took the reins from her. "An excellent job, Lady Darrow. I should like to see you with one of my own teams. Not many women have your skill."

"Thank you," Emily said, pleased that she had not lost her touch after so many years.

A cursory glance at the hamlet told Hart that there would be no food to tempt them, so with reluctance he urged the horses onward toward Luton. They could eat and arrive at the Grand Junction by late afternoon. And if luck was with them, there would be word about the boys awaiting them. Surely, if they had made for the canal, one of the Runners would find news of them. And if those two rascals had headed south, he could turn the carriage toward London immediately.

Hart wondered how long it had been since Lady Darrow had last visited London. It might be the very thing to bring a gleam of delight to her eyes. She would protest against the expense, but he would do his best to persuade her to let him treat her. He wanted to reward her for being such an amiable companion.

7

"What the deuce!" Hart exclaimed as the carriage rounded a blind corner. He yanked on the reins in a frantic attempt to halt the horses before they crashed into the roiling white mass that covered the road.

Emily grabbed for her bonnet and the side of the seat as the carriage skidded to a stop. Bleating sheep instantly surrounded the vehicle.

"Damn and blast!"

"It looks to be a smallish flock," Emily said soothingly. "We should not have to wait long until they move past."

"We should not have to wait at all," the duke snapped. He grabbed the reins with firm control as the horses danced uneasily, demonstrating their dislike for the small, noisy creatures. Hart looked about for any sign that there was someone tending the milling sheep, finally spotting a young boy at the far edge of the flock.

"You! Boy!" he called. "Get these blasted sheep out of the road."

The lad grinned and waved his stick at the sheep. They ignored him and remained scattered across the road.

Hart shoved the reins into Emily's hands and jumped to the ground. He waved his arms at the encroaching sheep. "Shoo! Scat!" The sheep remained impervious to his commands.

Emily convulsed in laughter.

Hart spun around, glaring. "What is so funny?" he demanded.

She pressed her hand to her mouth, stifling her giggles. "Nothing."

The duke waded into the milling mass that covered the road from hedge to hedge. As quickly as he chased one sheep behind the carriage, another would change direction and charge back toward him.

"Damn animals!"

"Perhaps if I drive the carriage forward slowly they will move aside ..."

"You are an expert on sheep?" he asked sarcastically.

"I know that they will often not do what you wish them to," she said. "Perhaps you could stand by the near horse's head, so he will not be frightened."

Hart scowled darkly but did as she suggested. Emily snapped the reins and the carriage lurched forward, the restive horses eager to free themselves from the annoying animals blocking the road. Sheep darted out of the way as the curricle inched a path through the stubborn animals. The lad tending the sheep stood and watched their laborious progress as if it were the most fascinating thing he had ever seen.

At last, Emily guided the carriage past the thickest portion of the flock. Only a few stray sheep stood in their way. Hart directed a final irritated glance at the lad for doing such an ineffectual job of taking charge of his animals, then clambered back into the carriage.

"Thank you," he said abruptly, taking back the reins. With his face set in an angry scowl, he urged the horses into a sprightly trot.

"Do you always get so upset over minor delays?" she asked. "It was only a bunch of sheep."

Hart reined in the horses and twisted around to face her, his blue eyes once again icy with anger. "My son has been missing for nine days, Lady Darrow. I begrudge every single second that delays the search." He turned back and snapped the reins.

Emily felt chastened. She worried about Jeremy constantly, but she had not seen any signs of such worry in the duke—until now. She realized with sudden insight that his overbearing behavior and sour moods were not parts of his normal personality, but only the reflection of his deep worry. Because he had not vocalized it, she had not seen it before. His excessive anger at the inn in Hitchin was easily explained now. Emily's opinion of him rose several notches. They were not so very unalike after all. They were both parents, worried sick about their sons.

She wondered if his blustering about her reputation had been a cover for his own fears. Emily hoped it meant he was not really so loath to have her along on the chase.

They reached Luton without further delay. Hart pulled up before the first inn they saw. "We shall eat here," he told her as he assisted her from the carriage. "It should not take more than a few hours to reach the canal. There is plenty of daylight left."

Emily looked about the well-appointed inn with weary apprehension, instantly recognizing it as several steps above the manner of accommodations they had enjoyed in recent days. That meant it would be more expensive. And the duke's insistence on a private parlor did not decrease that expense. To her concern over Jeremy was added the increasing worry over money.

She could go home, she thought, but dismissed the idea as quickly as it had come. She would not rest until Jeremy was found, and traveling with the duke would mean she would receive the news quicker. Surely the bills for her food and lodging would not be too prohibitive. The money would be found somewhere.

They ate a hasty meal. The duke, still disturbed by the day's delays, was anxious to be on the road again, and his eagerness, combined with his hunger, caused him to dispatch his late luncheon in record time.

"I should like to allow you to rest," he said apologetically to her as he finished the last of his ale, "but I think we should depart forthwith."

Nodding, Emily hastened to finish her own meal. In a short time, she found herself seated beside him once again as the carriage raced out of town.

Emily cast the duke a look of surprise when he pulled up the carriage at a small crossroad, intent in his perusal of the signpost. "Are we lost?" she asked sweetly.

"Of course we are not lost," he said with indignation. "I am merely trying to decide which road will get us to our destination faster."

"What is our destination?"

Hart looked at her with unrestrained exasperation. "I told you, Lady Darrow, that we are making for Hemel Hempstead. It is the most direct route to the canal."

"I find it difficult to believe that all these meandering country lanes will get us there faster than the main road."

"The main road would have taken us miles out of our way," he explained with growing impatience.

"While your way only gets us lost."

"Since you are so superior at navigation, Lady Darrow, perhaps you would care to tell me which route we should take," he said with broad sarcasm.

"As neither sign indicates which route goes to Hemel Hempstead, I find that a rather difficult choice to make. However"—she darted him a lofty glance—"the sign says the village to the left is closer, so I suggest we take that road and ask for directions when we arrive."

"I rather think we should keep to the right," the duke said, carefully turning the carriage in that very direction. "We have been traveling southward; the canal should be due west of us by now."

Emily shook her head in frustration at the duke's pigheadedness.

Her frustration turned to gloating superiority when they arrived at the next village, only to be informed that they were traveling north, away from both the canal and Hemel Hempstead.

"I do not wish to hear one word from you, Lady Darrow," the duke said in a commanding tone as they drove away from the village.

Emily darted him a wounded glance. "Have I said anything?"

"Do not play injured innocence with me. I know what you are thinking."

"Oh, I see I can add prescience to the list of your many sterling qualities."

"Do not press me too far, Lady Darrow, or I might be tempted to deposit you at the next inn we pass."

"Assuming you can find it," she muttered under her breath, but flashed him a sweet smile. "I have every faith in your ability to get us to Hemel Hempstead, your grace."

The shadows were lengthening when they at last reached the placid waters of the Grand Junction.

Hart handed the reins to Emily and scrambled down the brush embankment until he reached the towpath. The surface of the canal was smooth, the June breeze creating only the faintest of ripples across the water. There was nary a boat in sight.

"Now that we are here, what are we to do?" Emily asked when he climbed back into the carriage.

"If there is any news, it will be at the inn in Tring," Hartford said. He looked down the canal, as if hoping for a glimpse of his son.

"Do you honestly believe they are still on their way to London?"

"No," he replied. "I think they are in London by this time. And heaven help us if they do not go to the house."

"Is your son well acquainted with the city? Will he know how to find your house?"

"He has been there enough times," Hart replied. "He knows the direction. If he can find it."

"Do you have any relatives or friends in London where he might go instead?" she asked.

Hart shook his head. "I doubt he would seek out Michellene," he said dryly.

"Michellene?" Emily looked at him in puzzlement.

"My mistress," Hart told her.

"Your son is acquainted with your mistress?" she asked, shocked at his bold disregard for the properties.

"We have taken her driving on occasion," Hart said.

Emily bit her lower lip to keep from telling the duke what she thought of a man who would allow his ten-year-old son to be in the company of his mistress. She might have been out of society for some length of time, but she did not think matters had changed that drastically. It suddenly made Hartford's reputation all the more disturbing.

"You are shocked," he said simply.

"Yes," she said. "It is bad enough that the young men learn of such things in their later years, but at his age!"

"I do not think he is cognizant of the nature of our relationship," Hart said with a wry grin. "To him, she is merely a pretty lady of my acquaintance, who likes to indulge him with sweets."

"In order to ingratiate herself with his father, no doubt," Emily said before she could stop herself.

Hart turned and looked at her with a steady gaze. "I realize this is perhaps a difficult subject for a woman to understand, but it is the way of the world."

"If you had a wife, I would not think you would be

so devil-may-care about your son's companions," she said icily.

"Perhaps not," he said, after a moment's pause. "But I do not have a wife, and I see nothing wrong in introducing him to a lady whose company I enjoy. I only hope that when he is ready for his own initiation, he can find someone as good-hearted as she."

"Perhaps you can save her for him," Emily said sarcastically. "Phillip surely will be ready for such an experience before too many more years pass."

"An excellent idea," Hart said. "I would be quite willing to take your son under my wing as well, when the time comes."

Emily gasped.

"Am I driving too fast for you, Lady Darrow?" Hart asked with a mischievous twinkle in his eye.

"You know very well it is not your driving," she said. "I must say, I expect a duke to be imperious, but your utter disregard for the proprieties stuns me."

"If anyone disregards the proprieties, Lady Darrow, it is you," he said. "It is a time-honored tradition for fathers to guide their sons through their initiation into the mysteries of sex. It is highly improper for a single lady to be traveling with an unrelated male."

"Our situation is totally respectable."

"We know that," he replied. "But you saw how Amberley leered. He certainly did not think it so."

"I do not care what he thinks. We are adults. You are talking about a mere child," she protested.

"And when do you suppose Stephen started to visit with the ladies?" he asked. "Fifteen? Sixteen?"

"I do not know," she answered stiffly.

"I was fifteen myself," said the duke. "But some have said I was a prodigy."

"I should think so," she said.

"How old were you when you first lay with a man?" he asked. "Seventeen? Eighteen?"

"Your grace!"

"You could not have been any older when you wed Stephen," he said with an unrepentant laugh.

"That does not give you leave to bring up the most private of matters," she said.

He shrugged. "I believe it was you who initiated this conversation."

"I asked if you might have some clue where the boys would go in London. I had no intention of discussing your mistress, your sexual prowess as a youth, or your plans for your own son's debauchment."

"Fair enough," said the duke with a smile. "I shall leave off discussing such *disturbing* matters. We will drive on to Tring and see if there are any messages from the Runners."

Emily thought it would take her all of those miles before her flaming cheeks returned to their normal color.

Never in her life had she indulged in such a warm conversation with a man, even her husband. What had come over her? She should have turned away and shown the duke the full measure of her disgust. Instead, she had goaded him into further outrageous revelations. And he had enjoyed every minute of it, taking great delight in seeing just how much he could shock her.

He had succeeded very well in his aim. If anything, she began to suspect, the duke's reputation was understated. He was no doubt the greatest libertine in the realm.

She almost smiled at the thought. Hart's behavior was most perplexing. He prosed on about propriety in one moment, then engaged her in the most inappropriate discussions in the next. He alternated between being overbearingly ducal and flirtatious and teasing. She did not know whether to be exasperated or laugh at the contrast.

Hart was a decidedly bad influence upon her. Every day they spent together made her life in Lincolnshire seem farther and farther away. Worries and responsibilities fled her mind with every mile they traveled. She had not felt so carefree in years, and it was all the fault of this roguish duke. He had reawakened a part of her she had long thought buried.

The situation would be amusing if the reason for their travel was not so critical. The thought of Jeremy quickly sobered her. How could she find any enjoyment in a journey with such a serious purpose? It seemed a traitorous reaction. Emily must not allow thoughts of Hartford to distract her from the more important purpose of finding her son.

Despite her resolution, Emily could not shake her curiosity about the duke's mistress. What did she look like? Was she lithe and blonde? Or a luscious brunette? An opera dancer or a professional courtesan? Did Hart visit her daily? Or only infrequently?

Emily firmly told herself to stop being so foolish. The duke's private life was none of her concern. She had no interest in it.

They crossed the canal and, with the help of the main road, arrived at Tring without further delay. Hart drew up in front of the small inn on the outskirts of the village and escorted her into a private parlor, then went to inquire about any messages.

Emily looked up with anxious eyes when he re-entered. "Is there any news?"

Hart shook his head wearily. "The men have scoured up and down the canal, but no one reports seeing two boys."

"Perhaps they are not going to London after all," she said.

He looked at her. "Ireland?"

"You know I have always thought that," she said.

"But which port? Bristol? Or Liverpool?"

"They have been heading steadily in a southwesterly direction," she reminded him.

"Yet why the canal map if they are not travelling the

Grand Junction?" he asked, puzzlement furrowing his brow.

"Perhaps it connects with some other canal that takes them to Bristol or Liverpool."

"I do not know." He frowned. "And I doubt there is anything like a map in this town. I will send messages on to the Runners to procure one and investigate that possibility." He sat down. "I think, Lady Darrow, that we would do well to remain here, at least for the night. Perhaps in the morning there will be more welcome news."

Emily nodded her assent. They had not traveled at a rocketing pace that day, yet she was as exhausted as if they had set a new traveling record. She had far too many new things to consider.

The changes in the duke had been mercurial. From excitement at knowing the boys had been at Hitchin to his biting anger at the poor service at the inn; from his ability to laugh at himself for the same incident to his fury at the sheep-caused delay; from his shockingly bold conversation to his obvious discouragement that there was no new sign of Jeremy and Phillip.

All conspired to make him much more human. He never lost his ducal manner of demanding arrogance, but Emily began to catch a glimpse of the man who lay beneath it. And however much the duke would likely protest, it appeared he was mortally human after all. She liked him all the more for it.

Phillip trudged down the country lane in a disconsolate manner. "How was I to know that Oxford would be so boring?"

"You said the same thing in Cambridge," Jeremy reminded him. "I said we should avoid it altogether."

"Well, at least you have a new shirt," said Philip.

"Which I wouldn't have needed if you hadn't been so pigheaded about going to Oxford in the first place," Jeremy pointed out.

"Let me see the map," Philip said, firmly determined to change the subject. He carefully unfolded the well-worn paper. "It's only a few more miles to Abingdon, I think."

"I hope so," muttered Jeremy. Apart from the dull trip to Oxford, he was consumed with jealousy over the bright new Belcher neckerchief that his friend had purchased in town. Jeremy would have given much to own so grand a thing, but concern over his dwindling supply of money stayed his hand. A lot of good a neckerchief would do them when they were forced to beg at farmhouses for something to eat.

"What if we cannot find a ride at Abingdon?" Phillip asked.

"Then we shall go further south to the Kennet-and-Avon," Jeremy replied. "They both will take us to Bath. There is no sense in walking all the way if we can catch a ride in Abingdon."

"I think we should have followed the river," Phillip said. "It would have been more interesting."

"And taken longer. Look at the map, silly. The river makes that huge loop. We'd have to go miles out of our way."

"I suppose you're right," mumbled Phillip.

Another hour brought them to the outskirts of Abingdon. They bought more food for their journey and wandered toward the river. They walked along the Thames for a while until they came to the lock connecting the Wilts-and-Berks canal to the river. To their intense pleasure, there were several narrow boats in the canal basin.

"Oh, boy!" Phillip shouted with glee. "We should be to Bristol in no time!"

Jeremy smiled at the outburst, but his heart also beat with excitement at the sight. It almost made it seem possible that they would reach their journey's end—or at least the next stage. He could practically picture the quay in Bristol, the Irish packet boat bobbing against the dock.

"Quick, let's find a boatman who will take us." Phillip started to run toward the bank of the canal.

"Wait a minute," Jeremy called after him. "We have to do this carefully, so they don't charge us for passage. We must make up a good story as to why we need to get to Bath."

"Our mother is ill?"

"And why are we not taking the mail?"

"Because we are very poor and could not afford it?" Phillip asked brightly.

"But if our mother is ill, would we not spend any amount necessary to rush to her side?" Jeremy asked. "Think of something else."

"Our grandfather," said Phillip eagerly. "He cut our papa off without a shilling because he married our mama, who was an actress, and now Papa is sick and we are going to Grandfather to ask him for money for some medicine."

"We are traveling too slow for it to be some dire emergency," Jeremy said. "How about our parents died and we are going to live with our grandfather?"

"And we need to travel on the canal so the authorities will not grab us and turn us over to the workhouse! A capital idea."

Jeremy shot a respectful glance at Phillip. It was a good touch. "Let's give it a try, then."

They walked toward the canal edge. Jeremy adopted a pose of studied nonchalance as he carefully eyed the men standing along the shore. Which one looked most likely to take on two passengers?

Before he could decide, Phillip darted ahead and ran up to the first boatman. "Can you take us to Bath?" he asked boldly.

"And what does a young whipper like yourself want with Bath?" the boatman demanded.

Jeremy stepped forward. "We are traveling to our grandfather's—he lives just outside Bath."

The man eyed them suspiciously. "Essent thee never yerd o' the mail? It's a mite faster than the canal."

"We cannot afford a seat on the mail," Phillip said.

The man squinted at them harder. "Not running away, are ye?"

"Oh, no, sir," Phillip replied in his most trustworthy manner. "It's just now, with Mama dead . . ." Real tears sprang to his eyes.

"Where's yer pa?" another boatman asked.

"He's in the Indies, with the army," Phillip improvised. "And he always told us we were to go to Grandfather's if anything should happen while he was gone."

The men exchanged looks.

"I got no cargo back t' the mines," one man said. He looked at the boys. "I cain't take ye all t' way to Bath, mind, but I can get you pretty near."

"Oh, thank you, sir," Phillip said.

"How long will it take?" Jeremy asked.

"Depends on how soon we starts," the man said. "You lads ready now?"

They nodded eagerly.

"I'll have the lad harness up the horse," he said. "You two know anything about horses?"

Phillip shook his head.

"Ah, well." The man shrugged.

"Which boat is yours?" Phillip asked.

The boatman pointed. "The end one."

"Can we go aboard now?" Jeremy asked.

"Suit yourself," the man said. "Mind, don't touch anything."

"Isn't this amazing?" Phillip asked as they scrambled aboard the long, narrow craft.

"Dirty is more like it," said Jeremy. "He's been hauling coal."

"I think I should like to be a boatman when I grow up," Phillip announced. "I could sail up and down the whole of England, carrying goods here and there. All the people in the towns would be glad to see me. I could sleep on the boat and even grow a beard!"

"They could call you the 'Mad Marquess,' " Jeremy said dryly.

"You could have a boat too, and be the 'Violent Viscount.' "

"I certainly don't want to run a canal boat when I grow up," Jeremy said. "I'm going to take my seat in the Lords and do something useful."

"Hauling cargo is useful," Phillip protested. "Probably more useful than sitting in the Lords. Papa says it is deucedly boring."

"That's probably because he doesn't care a fig about it," Jeremy said.

"He does care," Phillip argued.

"Then why is he always going to boxing matches and horse races and things?" Jeremy challenged him.

"Because ... because he's a duke! Dukes are supposed to do that sort of thing."

"He'd just rather do those sorts of things," Jeremy said. "It's all right, that's the sort of thing my papa liked, too."

"What's it like not having a papa?"

Jeremy shrugged. "It means you don't have much money," he said. "And no one to take you to boxing matches. It's not too bad, I guess. I could not imagine not having a mama."

"I think mothers are a nuisance," Phillip said. "They're always cosseting and fidgeting a fellow, from what I can tell. Just like a nursemaid, only worse. Papa doesn't bother with all that."

"You lads ready to go?" The boatman jumped aboard.

Phillip and Jeremy nodded, then watched with rapt fascination as the man untied the lines that held them to the shore.

"Now don't go jumping about," he cautioned. Sitting

on the stern, he pushed away from the bow of the next boat. The towline grew taut as the massive horse lumbered down the tow path. Jeremy watched with interest as the boat made its slow way down the canal. His reservations about the trip had faded over the last day, and now, with Bristol seeming so near, his anticipation grew. They were going to make it to Ireland yet.

Wouldn't his mother be surprised?

8

Emily awoke to the sound of rain splattering against the window of her tiny room at the Hare's Tail in Tring. It would be another miserable day of traveling. With a sigh, she rose and quickly dressed. She did not wish to keep Hartford waiting. Rain or no, he would be eager for an early start.

The duke was already in the dining parlor, looking with dismay at the enormous platter of food upon the table. Laden with ham, bacon, and broiled kidneys, it was surrounded by a huge basket of bread, a heaping tub of butter and a large jar of strawberry jam. Tea, coffee, and chocolate steamed in their pots.

Hart looked up when Emily entered the room and flashed her a grateful smile. "I am delighted to see you, Lady Darrow," he said. "I was sorely afraid I would have to eat all this myself."

"How many people did you tell the landlord were in our party?" she asked as she took her seat. "Ten?"

"I suspect they are trying to outdo themselves in entertaining their 'noble' guests."

"True," she replied, spreading jam over a thick slice of freshly baked bread. "I doubt dukes are an everyday occurrence in Tring."

"Good God, do you think I march into every inn and make myself known by name?" he asked. "I am not such a fool as all that. The man probably thinks I am merely an earl."

Emily lifted a skeptical brow but did not press the matter.

As the duke appeared to be in no hurry, Emily decided to treat herself to a slice of ham. Sated at last, she glanced at the duke, expecting him to be impatient to depart. But instead of displaying his usual restless edginess, he was staring out the window, his expression glum. "Do you not wish to leave soon?" Emily asked.

The duke turned away from his rapt contemplation of the tracks of rain dripping down the window. "Where do you suggest we go, Lady Darrow?"

Emily stared at him with growing surprise. "You do not plan to continue the search today?"

The duke shook his head. "Where would we look? They have disappeared," he said, then caught himself at her look of horror. "Not literally, of course. It is only that they have not been seen recently. I am certain they are quite all right."

It was an obvious attempt to reassure her, but to Emily his words lacked conviction. "They were last seen in Hitchin on Monday!" Her voice rose with desperation. "That was three days ago."

"It took us longer than that to locate them the first time," the duke said in a soothing tone. "I am certain we will get another clue to their trail soon. After all, I must have half the men in England on their track."

Although she nodded at his words, Hart did not think she was overly convinced. He stood and walked to the windows. Rubbing at the mist on the glass, he peered out onto the rain-swept lane of mud that lay outside. Perhaps the rain would stop this afternoon and they could venture out.

Damn this weather. He darted a quick glance at Lady Darrow. She looked so calm and composed, sitting there sipping her tea. He knew she was worried to death, yet she rarely gave any outward indication of her feelings. She had a serenity of acceptance that he found disturbing.

He could not decide from one moment to the next whether he was glad of her company or wished her to Jericho—or at least back to Lincolnshire. Despite her flashes of apprehension over the fate of her son, she remained entirely too self-assured and controlled. That unnerved him—almost as much as it fascinated him. She had held up against circumstances that would have wilted any number of women of his acquaintance, and endured this miserable chase with a disregard for her own comfort that amazed him.

Not that she was uncomplaining. But it seemed that her complaints were directed primarily at him rather than at their manner of travel. Yesterday, for example, when she disagreed with him over which lane to take. It had not helped at all to discover that she was right.

Lady Darrow had been managing things on her own for far too long. It was an unfortunate trait of widows. A pity she had not found refuge with her family, where she could have handed her burdens over to another. By managing on her own, she had become insufferably independent.

While he had nothing against independent women, Hart saw nothing attractive about them either. Independent women were too prone to speak their own minds, disagree, and make life generally miserable for those around them. Fortunately, they were such uncommon creatures that he rarely had to worry about them. The numerous ladies who had been under his protection at one time or another had not minded bowing to his wishes. He found their acquiescence much more pleasant than Lady Darrow's headstrong ways. But he could certainly tolerate her company until the boys were found. After all, he was a magnanimous man.

* * *

By mid-morning, Emily thought she would scream if the duke crossed the room and peered out the window one more time. He must have made the trip more than fifty times in the last hour. His restlessness was infectious, yet she was determined to resist its influence. It would accomplish nothing. He was the one who had decided to wait for further news before hastening out in the rain. Why could he not be content with his decision?

"I am going to go outside and check the weather," the duke announced abruptly, and left the room before she could even acknowledge his declaration.

Did Hartford think the rain would stop miraculously if he commanded it? Emily laughed inwardly. He probably did, and with some justification. She suspected there was very little on earth that could withstand the duke's determined nature. Or very little on earth that the duke did not think he could command.

She wondered briefly what it would be like to know that you were one of the most powerful persons in the country, with an army of servants at your bidding, surrounded by yes-sayers and toad-eaters who would never thwart your desires. Had the duke ever once found someone who would not bend to his will? Probably not. If he could not win someone over by force of command, he could always dangle money as an enticement. Emily was not even positive *she* could resist this combination of power and wealth if he ever decided to use its full force upon her. She was grateful he had not done so.

Hartford returned in a few minutes, dashing droplets of water from his coat.

"Still raining?" Emily asked with a hint of amusement. Perhaps his influence was not so great after all.

"Yes," he said curtly.

The landlord appeared at the door. "Will you be wishing luncheon, your lordship?" he asked, rubbing his hands in pleasurable anticipation of further custom.

"Yes, please," said Emily, ignoring the duke's frown at her presumption.

They ate their meal in comparative silence, the duke pointedly concentrating on his food. Emily chose not to notice his forced absorption. If he did not wish to make conversation, it was nothing to her. Yet she found his restless silence as unnerving as his earlier pacing.

Throwing down his napkin, the duke suddenly jumped to his feet. "This is ridiculous!" he exclaimed. "The rain is slackening. I am going to have the horses put to."

"Where are we to go?" she asked.

"I cannot sit here any longer doing nothing," he said. "We will backtrack to the canal, and talk to everyone we encounter."

"There will likely be few people out in weather such as this."

"You are more than welcome to remain here, Lady Darrow."

"I only fear we will learn little. Did not the Runners already search this stretch of the canal?"

"They may have missed something," the duke insisted. "We should have had some news by now."

"Unless, of course, the boys are nowhere near the canal."

"And where do you think they have gone?" he asked sarcastically. "The antipodes?"

"The Grand Junction is not the most direct route to either Liverpool or Bristol," she said.

The duke turned disdainful eyes upon her. "There you are, going on about Ireland again. Do you honestly believe that your son is so stupid as to wish to travel clear to Ireland over the trifling issue of some fairies?"

"May I remind you that your son is along on this journey as well."

"They are going to London," he said definitely.

"Then why have they not arrived there yet?" she

asked. "There has been no message coming from your house announcing their appearance."

The duke frowned. "This waiting is pointless. I should be out looking for them."

"To what purpose?" she asked. "You have no idea of their direction."

"And I certainly will not get any idea of it if I stay locked up in this inn all day."

"When are the Runners to contact you again?"

"They will send news whenever they have some."

"And how are they to convey their message if you are not here to receive it?" she asked. "If you go gallivanting about the countryside, you might put even more distance between yourself and your son."

The duke's frown turned to a scowl. "So you think we should cool our heels and wait here until the cobwebs form around our shoes?"

"I see little point in racing about to no purpose. What you propose is a total waste of time and effort. As you previously pointed out to me—leave the search to the professionals."

"And you yourself are such an expert on these matters that you can advise me?" he sneered.

"I do know that there is little need of action merely for action's sake," she replied in a calm, even voice. "Something you, like my late husband, seem to be particularly obtuse about understanding."

"Trust a woman to advocate no action at all," Hart muttered.

"What I am advocating is not indulging in wasteful folly just to appease your conscience," she said, her anger growing.

"Whatever does my conscience have to do with it?" he demanded.

"Surely, as a parent, you must feel some responsibility for your son's aberrant behavior?"

He stared at her with an incredulous expression on his face. "There is no question that *you* must bear the brunt of the responsibility for your son's actions," he said. "What can one expect when you fill a child's head with such nonsense? But to accuse me—"

"I did not accuse you of anything," Emily protested.

"The deuce you didn't." The duke's face was livid. "You as good and came out and said it was my fault Phillip ran away."

"Why do you always persist in misinterpreting everything I say?" she asked.

"Perhaps because you say things in such a way that your meaning is unclear."

"I was merely trying to say that *if* you had any worries that there was something you did that ultimately encouraged Phillip to run away, dashing out on a fool's errand is not going to make the situation better."

Hart glowered. "And what, precisely, is it that I did to make my son run away from school?"

"That question from a man who allows a young child to meet with his mistress?"

"Lady friend," the duke insisted.

"A father who is too busy to read stories to his son?" she persisted. "A father who perhaps has little patience to answer the importuning questions of a curious lad?"

"I am not his tutor," the duke growled. "I am his father."

"What precisely do you do with Phillip when you are together?"

"I take him places," the duke said with a defensive air. "Why, this spring we went to a rousing mill."

"A highly educational experience for a lad of ten," Emily said scornfully.

"At least the boy will be well versed in the customary actions of men," he retorted. "I suspect your son's greatest ambition is to grow up and find a nice lady to cosset and coddle him just as his mama does."

"I do not cosset him," Emily protested.

"I can only imagine. How many sporting events has he seen? Has he ever come home with a torn pants leg or a bloody nose? You probably keep him wrapped up in cotton wool."

"I do not!" But at the back of her mind were the first niggling misgivings that perhaps she had been a bit overprotective of Jeremy.

The duke watched her with a growing sense of superiority. "I see my words have taken root," he said triumphantly.

"I dare you to show me where Jeremy's upraising has been in any way deficient to Phillip's." Emily set her mouth in a determined line, forcing her doubts away.

"Wait until we find them," Hart said. "I think the differences will be obvious."

Emily fixed him with an indignant look.

"Now, do not rise up in the boughs, Lady Darrow. I am certain you have done your best. But a boy needs a man's influence while he is growing up."

"I cannot see that your influence has been of much advantage to your son," she snapped. "In fact, there are many who would say that you have been highly remiss in exposing him to the less-savory aspects of life at such a young age."

"Good God, he is a boy, not an old woman. He'll learn about those things soon enough. Better from his father than from a bunch of misinformed cronies at school."

"It is a wonder you did not send him to Eton," she said. "I understand such *manly* 'subjects' are studied assiduously there. He would receive a much more thorough education than he could in Norfolk."

"You," said the duke, "are an ill-advised, interfering, and annoying woman. Would to God I had left you in Cambridge. Or Newmarket. Or better yet, in Norfolk."

"A typical response from one who cannot stand to be bested in an argument," she said tartly. "An attack is the best defense."

The duke shot her an angry look and abruptly left the parlor.

Emily was so furious that she could not sit still. She jumped to her feet and paced across the room, much as the duke had done earlier.

What an arrogant, infuriating man! He was so certain of his own infallibility he would not listen to any word of criticism or chastisement. He embodied all the worst characteristics of the male species: he was opinionated, arrogant, filled with self-importance, patronizing, and obtuse. And she had foolishly cast herself into a position of near-total dependence on him while they searched for their sons.

Emily felt once more that she was being pushed into a corner. It was like her father and uncle all over again—telling her what she should do, discounting her opinions, and berating her for her decisions. That had been one of the most joyous parts of her marriage with Stephen—he had not told her what to do or how to do it. Now that she had experienced that delicious freedom, she would never go back to male tyranny. She would never bow to the duke, no matter how strong his will.

Then reason dawned and Emily laughed. The duke was not threatening her with anything. He was not proposing to take over her life. He might criticize the manner in which she was raising Jeremy, but it mattered little—he had no say in what she could do. It was not as if she would have any contact with him after the boys were returned to school. She could endure his blustering opinions for the moment. After all, he was helping her find her son. She had to be grateful to him for that.

Yet deep down Emily was filled with disquiet. The duke's words bothered her more than she cared to admit. Not because they were right, but because of what they told her about him. He was not like Stephen. In the last two days, her rigid disapproval of Hart had be-

gun to waver. However, it was once again clear that he
was not at all the type of man she wanted anything to
do with. Hartford thought that all women should be
docile and subservient. She prayed they would find
Jeremy soon, so she could escape from his domineering ways.

Ignoring the chilling rain, Hart stomped down the
muddy lane that marked the center of Tring.

He knew it had been a mistake to take Lady Darrow
along on this chase, and her quarrelsome attitude today
only proved it. Who was she to criticize the way he
raised Phillip? He was doing exactly as he ought—and
correcting the mistakes of his own father in the bar-
gain. Phillip would never doubt that his father held him
in affection, or valued him more than the latest paint-
ing he had acquired. He did his best to avoid the rigidity he had so hated in his sire—the rigidity that had
been perpetuated at the detested Eton. Not pampering
the boy did not mean he did not love him.

Women had such funny ideas. Simply because he did
not indulge in open displays of affection or participate
in the silly rituals of childhood did not mean he was an
indifferent parent. Women were much too apt to put
emphasis on show rather than substance. Hart should
know—had not he discovered that about his own wife?

Lady Darrow was in no position to criticize him.
Granted, she had probably done an admirable job given
the circumstances of her situation. But no woman
alone could hope to raise a son properly. He was firmly
convinced the young viscount would be a plaguey
"mama's boy" for the remainder of his life. Poor
Stephen would be rolling in his grave if he should see
such a thing.

The duke paused, looking back up the lane at the
small cluster of buildings that was Tring. Perhaps he
could exert some influence upon Lady Darrow while
they were together, to show her the error of her ways

and impress upon her the course she needed to follow with Jeremy. It was really the least he could do for his old friend. Stephen would want him to make certain his son turned out the right way.

Of course, first they had to find those blasted boys. And while it chafed at him, Hart had to admit Lady Darrow was right on one score. All his frantic chasing about Norfolk in the first days after Phillip's disappearance had showed him that aimless effort, while it might make him feel useful, accomplished nothing. The Runners were trained to track their men—or boys—and it was laughable to think he could do better than the professionals. But the thought of spending days marooned at this tiny inn grated on his desire for quick results.

They were bound to hear something soon. And Lady Darrow was correct—he needed to be here when the news arrived. There was no telling what the news would be, and he might have to make some quick decisions. Best that he be at a place where the Runners could find him, and where he could dispatch them to do his bidding.

He wondered how he was going to explain his change in view to Lady Darrow when he returned to the inn. It would most likely be a repeat of yesterday—no open condemnation of his actions, but a broad glint of "I told you so" in her eyes.

Well, he did not need to be afraid of her. He was the Duke of Hartford, after all, and the opinion of a humble widow mattered little to him. He did not need unqualified adulation from every woman he met. Least of all from her.

9

By the time he returned to the inn, the duke was decidedly damp. He was glad of it, however, for it meant he could slip up to his room to change into dry clothing without first having to face Lady Darrow.

He was rather embarrassed by his earlier outburst. They had been squabbling like recalcitrant schoolchildren. Never mind that she managed to prick his pretensions as few others dared. He was a duke, and need not stoop to such petty argumentation. It was quite out of character for him. He rarely argued with anyone.

Of course, he was forced to admit that was mostly due to the fact that few people had the audacity to argue with him. It was one thing for which he could credit Lady Darrow—she certainly was not impressed by his rank or position. She raked him over the coals as if he were the lowliest stable boy.

It was merely one more reason he did not like women who were filled with an independent spirit. They were entirely too inclined to express their own opinions—and disagree with his. It was not something he deliberately sought. He much preferred women who were amiably complacent. In and out of bed.

He wondered whether Lady Darrow had been so assertive when she first married Stephen. Or had it been the years of impoverished widowhood that had so sharpened her tongue and her combative nature? By running the estate, she had taken on a task outside the usual sphere of a woman's duties. It was enough to have wrought a change in the most demure female. Hart laughed to himself. He doubted Lady Darrow had ever been demure.

Whatever the origin of her combative ways, they needed to reach some manner of accommodation if they were to continue together on the search for their sons. He reflected again that, despite his earlier reservations about journeying with her, Lady Darrow had proved to be a good traveler. He was not callous enough to abandon her in such an out-of-the-way place either. He would have to smooth things over enough so they could tolerate each other for the remainder of the search.

Hart only hoped they found those boys quickly. Before Lady Darrow had the opportunity to prick any more of his pretensions.

The longer the duke remained absent, the more embarrassed Emily became over her behavior. She had no right to lash out at him like that—what did she really know about him, or the kind of father he was? She had made sweeping generalizations based on nothing more than her own biased impressions of him.

She would not blame him a bit if he left her here, although she did not think he would. Perhaps he had decided to go out and search the area further, as he had wanted to. Who was she to criticize his desire for action? This forced inactivity wore on her as well.

But he angered her so when he put on his patronizing airs and treated her like a recalcitrant child. She was tired of being regarded as a less-than-complete person simply because she was a woman. Lord knows, she did a much better job of managing the estate than Stephen ever had. But since it was not something she was supposed to be good at, no one cared. Or worse, thought less of her for it.

Then the duke had the audacity to criticize her for the one area of her life of which people approved—her role as mother. She was willing to admit that Hart was a decent father—he did seem to be more interested in his son's life than many other men she had known. But still, he saw it all through the wrong end of a telescope. He used servants and tutors to deal with his son on a day-to-day basis. There was no question that the duke had never changed a nappy or held the basin for a desperately sick child. And by not so doing, he had missed one of the most important parts of parenthood. No amount of arguing would ever convince him of that, but she knew the truth of the matter. Because of that, she could feel the slightest bit of pity for him.

That thought brought a small smile to her face. Hartford would probably be appalled to think that anyone could find something to pity in his life. Dukes were not often thought to be pitiable creatures. But when their exalted position removed them from the joys of ordinary life, they were more to be pitied than envied. Despite all the hardships and suffering, Emily did not think she would wish to trade her life for his. She felt secure in her quiet, circumscribed world.

She heard the door open and she looked up, startled, as the duke walked into the room.

"Lady Darrow." He inclined his head in a brief greeting. "May I join you?"

Emily nodded. She waited for the duke to seat himself, then took a deep breath. "Your grace," she began.

"Hart."

"Hart." Emily fixed her gaze upon him. "I regret my cross words of this morning. I have no right to judge you."

The duke waved a dismissive hand. "I am guilty of the same crime," he said. "Do not think on it another moment. This blasted weather would drive a saint to sin."

"And I am certainly no saint," Emily said faintly, almost to herself.

The duke laughed. "'Tis something I have never been accused of either," he admitted.

They lapsed into an uneasy silence, punctuated only by the occasional crack and spark of the fire.

"This is madness," the duke said, rising from his chair. "Since the weather will force us to remain indoors for a time, we must find something with which to occupy ourselves. Do you play cards, my lady?"

Emily responded with a broad smile. "Indeed I do, your grace."

"I shall see if our genial landlord has a deck of cards." Hart strode across the small room.

It was some time before the duke returned, carrying a rather greasy and well-worn pack. "Not a new deck, by any means," he said apologetically. "But it will have to do. This is not Brooke's, after all."

"Is that where you play?" Emily asked. Stephen had belonged to Brooke's.

"Occasionally," he replied. "I rather prefer private games in the homes of friends. Club life grows boring after a time." He sat down and shuffled the cards. "Piquet seems most appropriate for the two of us. Will that do?"

"What stakes do you propose?"

"You are a gambler, are you, Lady Darrow?" he asked in a teasing tone.

A faint blush dusted her cheeks. "I had not meant we should play for money. Real money, at least. But even pretend money makes things more exciting. Stephen and I would play for outlandish imaginary stakes."

"And who usually won?" Hart asked as he dealt out the cards.

"We were evenly matched."

That said a great deal, Hart thought. Stephen might have squandered money on horses and trinkets, but he was not a bad card player. Which meant Lady Darrow would be a tolerable opponent. The thought pleased him. The duke enjoyed a challenge.

"A pound a point, Lady Darrow?"

"Do call me Emily," she said. "It seems rather foolish to maintain such formality after all these days."

"Emily," he repeated. "A nice name. It suits you. From the Latin, is it not?"

"Stephen said it was either Greek or Latin," she replied as she studied her cards. "Having neither language, I did not much care."

"At least your parents showed some sense in naming you. I shall bear the scar of my name till the day I die."

"Oliver is not so awful."

"You do not know the half of it. Oliver Cromwell Elliott."

Emily could not stifle a giggle. The duke shot her a dampening look, the impact of which was broken by his following grin.

"What a horrible thing to do to a child," she said. "Did your parents ever explain why?"

"My father had a rather perverse view of history," he said. "I tried to ask him about it several times, but he never gave me an answer."

"I can see why you named your son Phillip. I am sure that has spared him no end of agony at school."

"Indeed," he agreed. "Is Jeremy a family name?"

"No. Stephen and I both liked it for precisely that reason."

The duke rearranged the cards in his hand. "Are you ready to begin?"

"Yes indeed." Emily fixed him with a challenging stare.

She was more than a match for him, the duke was forced to admit after they had played several hands. Less than ten pounds separated their winnings.

He watched intently as she dealt the next round. She had beautiful hands, he noted, with long, slim, tapering fingers. Elegant hands. Lady's hands. Except where they were reddened and work-roughened. A startling spurt of anger surged through him. Emily's hands should be pale and soft, set to tasks no more demanding than embroidery or playing the pianoforte. Yet there was no question she was forced to work at jobs more suited to a housemaid.

What onerous duties had she been compelled to perform in the name of survival? Cooking and cleaning were probably the least of them. She probably had very little household help. He cringed at the thought of Emily emptying out coal scuttles and scrubbing the entry hall.

He felt an unfamiliar disquietude that in his homes such daily chores were performed by an army of servants. His wife had never exerted herself to do anything more strenuous than ringing for tea during their entire marriage. A life such as Emily led would have killed Louisa as surely as childbirth had.

Hart glanced at Emily with newfound admiration. Despite her change of fortune, she did not seem bowed or cowed by the reversals life had dealt her. If anything, he suspected they had strengthened her. It was the quality he admired most, her strength. Lesser women would have given up long ago. But she clung to her goal of hanging on to the estate for her son. He damn well hoped Jeremy appreciated all his mother was doing for him. When they found those miserable brats, he would be sure to make a few things clear to the young viscount.

"Contemplating your debts?"

Emily's teasing voice jarred him back to awareness. "I should have known better than to play cards with Stephen's wife," he said as he examined the cards in his hands. A miserable holding again. Then a thought struck him. "Shall we play for real stakes, Emily? Perhaps the challenge will improve my play."

Emily folded her cards and laid them on the table. "Those who need the spur of real losses to inspire their

zeal for cards have the gambling fever," she said
curtly. "I have no wish to encourage any such thing."

Hart knew that she would be insulted if he explained
his real motive. It would not be too difficult for him to
miss a point here and there, and she could end up with
a tidy sum by the end of play. Yet she was far too full
of pride to accept such a deliberate gesture from him,
if she suspected his motive. "I assure you, I suffer
from no such malady." He tossed his own cards down
and walked to the window again. "I must concede your
skill at play, my lady."

The rain had stopped for the most part, but a light,
misting drizzle kept the day solidly gray. They were
certainly doomed to spend the night here again. He
turned and faced the room. "Surely, it must be time for
dinner," he said. "Are you hungry?"

Emily smiled. "Without any activity more draining
than cards, it is not easy to work up an appetite. But do
order food if you wish."

Hart did so. If he could not advance money to her
through card play, he could at least feed her. This
might be a modest country inn, but the food was good.
Emily could stand to put on a little more flesh. Not
that she was unpleasantly thin, but more rounded
curves would not be amiss.

The weather the following morning was in no way
better than the previous day's. Hart lingered as long as
he could over breakfast, but even so, the long hours of
the day stretched out before him. Restlessly, he criss-
crossed the private parlor.

"Do stop your pacing," Emily said with exasperation. "It is driving me mad."

"So is this enforced wait," the duke snapped.

"Perhaps the landlord has some reading material.
Something that will soothe your temper."

"A book of improving sermons, no doubt." The duke
snorted his disinterest.

"Which might do you some good," Emily observed with a pointed look. She went in search of the innkeeper, and returned forthwith with several tattered volumes.

"You are in luck," she said. "Some impoverished tutor left these in partial payment for his rooms."

"Oh, good." The duke grimaced. "Latin grammars? Or higher mathematics?"

"English history and Cobbett's *Rules of Grammar.*" The duke shuddered.

"I thought you might prefer the history," she said, handing him the book.

"Read it to me," he said, resigned to a dull morning. But anything was better than sitting here staring at each other in silence for hours on end. Pray to God that the weather would improve soon.

"Shall I start with the Civil War?" Emily asked impishly. She laughed aloud at the duke's withering look.

"Anything but that," he said as he flung himself into a chair.

Emily began with the tale of the Norman conquest under William. Before she had reached the Wars of the Roses, the duke was asleep. Obviously, he was not a student of history.

Closing the book and setting it on the table, Emily sat quietly in her chair and took the opportunity to study him carefully. It would not take much imagination to perceive that he was an aristocrat. Despite the fact that even he was beginning to look a little worse for wear after such harried travel, there was no mistaking the expensive and elegant cut of his clothes—and the carelessly graceful way he wore them.

She was impressed that the duke traveled without his valet and a retinue of assistants. Emily admired self-reliance in a man, and he certainly was demonstrating it. She wondered if he even polished his own boots at night—but that might be too much to expect for a duke. Still, apart from his outburst about the food in

Hitchin, he had not complained overmuch about accommodations that were certainly well below the
standards to which he was accustomed.

There were lines of weariness etched in his face that
had not been there a week ago. Somehow, they made
him less forbidding. More beguiling. It made it easier
to remember that he was, when all was said, a very
worried parent. Just like her.

She looked at the hands that lay loosely atop his
legs. They were strong, masculine hands. She had an
impulse to reach out and touch them, to draw some of
that strength for herself. She was in sore need of it.

Even asleep he exerted a powerful male attraction.
She had wondered, when they first met, why women
were so drawn to him. Now she began to understand.
It was his *presence* that drew them like moths to the
flame. She had been dazzled by the light of it herself.
Even slumped in his chair, rumpled and weary, Emily
thought he was one of the most alluring men she had
ever met. He was demanding, exasperating, impatient,
and impulsive—all characteristics she normally disliked. But in him, the traits seemed appropriate. He
was a duke, after all. His attitudes were as much a part
of him as his blond hair or piercing blue eyes.

Emily closed her eyes and leaned back in her chair.
What was it that drew a woman to a man? With
Stephen, it had been his sense of fun, his cheerfulness,
and his smile. Not, she thought ruefully, sufficient rec-
ommendations for a mate. Had she to do it all over
again, she would certainly have searched for stability
most of all. Not the most romantical of notions, but a
very practical one.

She would not say that Hartford possessed that
quality—he was impetuous and volatile in nature. The
duke certainly did exactly as he pleased. Because of
his wealth he could afford such an attitude, while
Stephen could not.

Yet Hartford's worry over his son showed that he

had a softer side. He was a caring, compassionate father. He might indulge his son at times, but he did it for the right reason—not to earn love, but to show it.

Did he treat the women in his life with such tender care as well?

As soon as the thought came to her, Emily laughed inwardly at her silliness. Next she would be spinning schoolgirl dreams about the duke. And he was no white knight to ride up on his charger and rescue her. She knew that those sort of men only existed in fairy tales. It was enough that he permitted her to accompany him on the search for the boys. For a few days she was free of Longridge, free of her ordinary life. Free of everything except her worry over Jeremy.

Emily and the duke spent a desultory afternoon playing cards and talking. Before dinner, the landlord lighted the fire, which served to remove some of the damp from the room. After the meal, Emily gathered her needle and thread and applied herself to some necessary repairs.

Hart leaned back in his chair, one foot balanced on the fender. To think that one needed a roaring fire in June to keep warm! Such was England. He shifted the glass of brandy from hand to hand while he stared at the flames. When would they get more news about the boys?

He had been so certain that the boys had been making for the Grand Junction—and London. It was still possible. They could be in the metropolis at this very moment—although why two small boys with a minimum of pocket money would wish to be on their own in that city when they could have all the luxury of his London townhouse at their disposal mystified him.

Unless, of course, Phillip was afraid of the reception he would receive at Hartford House when his adventure became known. Hart was not a harsh disciplinarian, but he did not tolerate unbridled mischief in his son either. Yet he did not think fear kept Phillip away.

But if they had not gone to London, where would they go? He glanced quickly at Lady Darrow. She was still insistent that they were making their way to Ireland. The idea still seemed ridiculous to him. No lads their age would truly believe in the existence of leprechauns—not to the extent that they would traipse across the entire island and across the sea to prove or disprove their theories.

But they had been heading steadily westward ever since they left school. Perhaps something else drew them to Ireland? What was Phillip's passion?

Horses. The moment the thought sprang into his head, it all began to make sense. The visit to his stables at Newmarket. Phillip loved to accompany him to the races, to discuss bloodlines and breeding and the merits of this and that horse. He knew that Ireland was famous for its horses—indeed, Hartford had purchased several Irish mares only last year. Was Phillip planning to visit the horse breeders?

It was a likely possibility. It filled the duke with a vast sense of relief; if the boys were heading to Ireland, at least they were doing it for a rational reason. *If* they were going to Ireland. He was still not ready to accept that as their destination. They were not yet even halfway to the western coast. Those brats could have veered off in any direction after leaving Hitchin. It would be folly to anticipate their route of travel without more clues.

Hart dared a quick glance at Emily, whose head was bent intently over her sewing. He was glad he had dispatched men to scour the docks in Liverpool and Bristol, just in case. Hart discovered he had an excessive desire to see the smile on Emily's face when he located her son.

*   *   *

The next day was as bright and sunny as the previous two had been wet and cold. Despite his need for action, Hart knew it was pointless to aimlessly continue the search. Traveling further could only put him miles in the wrong direction when the next word of his son's whereabouts arrived.

An early-morning message arrived from one of the Runners, delineating the progress made—the towns visited and the routes inspected. There was no definite news. A few people thought they might have seen two boys, but no one came close to an official identification.

The rumor that most intrigued Hart placed the boys in Oxford only two days ago. Was it possible they were that close? He wished the woman could have been more definite in her identification. Hart scribbled hasty instructions to scour Oxford with more care. Lord knows what those two could have been doing there, but it was the only slim lead they had. Someone else in that town might have seen them.

He was relieved when Emily came down for breakfast. "The weather is better today," he announced with a cheerful smile.

"Do you plan to remain here still?"

He nodded. "There are some rumors, but nothing definite to report. I do not wish to go north, west, or south until we have a definite lead."

"More cards and English history?" she asked with a teasing smile.

"I think the improvement in the weather gives us a few more options." he said. "A short drive, or a walk perhaps, would alleviate some of the tedium."

"I realized during the night that highly unlikely as it is, should they decide to go to Lincolnshire, we shall have no way of knowing. I should dispatch a letter home."

"I sent a man to your house in case of that eventuality," the duke said. "They will get word to us no matter where we are. I always keep London and the Runners apprised of our location."

Emily marveled at his efficiency. Of course, with his vast resources, it was not a particularly difficult task. Money made everything easier. "I should like to take a drive, if you are willing," she said. She uttered a small laugh. "I fear I have become too accustomed to traveling. Sitting for two days seems an inordinate strain."

"I quite agree with you," Hart said. "Eat your breakfast and I shall arrange for the horses. We will see what the lovely countryside around Tring has in store for us."

Emily smiled at him with such eagerness that all memories of the two previous sodden days fled from his mind.

10

Tired of sitting in the dirty, narrow boat, Phillip strolled along the towpath as the canal cut across the Wiltshire countryside.

"Do you like working on the canal?" Phillip asked the lad guiding the tow horse.

He shrugged. "Don't know anything else."

"I think it would be exciting," Phillip said. "There is so much to see."

"Not after you've walked the same route a hundred times over," the boy complained. "But one day I'll have my own boat and then I won't have to keep to this canal. I'll go everywhere—even down to London."

"London is jolly fun," Phillip admitted. "Have you ever been there?"

The boy shook his head.

"I rather wish we were on our way there instead of Ireland," Phillip said in a confiding tone. "There is so much more to do in London."

"Why are you going to Ireland?"

Phillip nodded toward Jeremy, who was involved in deep conversation with the boatman.

"That's where *he* wanted to go."

"I thought you said you were going to Bath, to your grandfather's."

Phillip started guiltily, remembering their story. "Well, that is where we are going first. But we have an uncle in Ireland and this is probably where they will send us."

"Don't like the Irish," the boy announced.

"I've never met anyone from Ireland," said Phillip. "Why don't you like them?"

"Just don't," said the boy. "Don't like Frenchies neither."

"I don't care for them either," said Phillip. "We have to learn French at school and I don't like it at all."

"Maybe your grandfather won't make you go to school no more."

"You think so?" Phillip adopted a brightening look.

As they approached the holding pond for one of the numerous locks on the canal route, Phillip stepped back to allow the boy to tend to the horse. Other boats were pulled up in the catch basin, waiting for the eastbound boats to make their passage through the locks. Phillip clambered back into the boat when it pulled in alongside the others.

"You know, I think we'd do a lot better to leave the canal and strike out on our own," Jeremy whispered to his companion when he was settled in the hold.

"Whyever would you want to do that?" Phillip asked.

"Because these boats go so blasted slow," Jeremy explained. He unfolded their tattered map. "We've been on the canal for two days and we're barely past Swindon. At this rate, it will take us three more days to even reach Bath."

"We couldn't go any faster walking," Phillip said. "And you won't let us spend any money for the coach."

"We probably can't even get a coach going to Bath or Bristol from around here," Jeremy said. "But we might be able to get a ride with some farmer."

"And what if we don't? I do not want to walk all the way to Bristol."

"I bet we could walk faster than this boat is going. It must take an hour at least to get through each of these locks. If we went directly south, we could reach the Bath road. We're bound to find someone who would give us a ride."

"What does it matter how soon we get to Bristol?" Phillip asked. "Traveling this way isn't costing us much money, and that's what you're always so worried about."

"Yes, but we do have to go home eventually," Jeremy pointed out. "The longer we are gone, the more people are going to worry."

"I don't want to get back until after school term is ended," Phillip said. "Then we won't have to make up all the work."

"Elston probably won't even take us back," said Jeremy glumly. Now that the thrill of their adventure was wearing off, he began to think of the repercussions of their actions. He had the guilty feeling that his mother might be worried about him.

"So? I'd be glad to be out of school." Phillip grinned at the thought.

"Your papa would just hire you a tutor and keep you at home," Jeremy said. "Think of how boring that would be."

"True," Phillip admitted. He looked across the basin at the other narrow boats. "Still, isn't this a wonderful way to travel? It cannot be taking us more than a day or two longer than it would be if we caught a ride with someone. There's no guarantee of that, you know."

"You're right." Jeremy frowned at the truth of his words. "Well, we can keep to the canal for a while, at least. But we will have to hurry when we get closer to Bath."

"Oh, we shall," Phillip assured him, lying back against the hull to watch the clouds scud overhead.

"Do you think your father is worried about you?" Jeremy asked.

Phillip thought for a moment. "Maybe a little," he admitted. "But I bet not nearly as much as your mama. See—one more reason why mothers are a nuisance.

She's probably having fits of the vapors and is spending her days weeping hysterically over the loss of her precious son."

"Mama's not like that," Jeremy said. "She's never had a fit of vapors in her life. At least, I've never seen one." His face clouded. "Still, I bet she is worried."

"You know you're fine, so that's that," Phillip said.

"I wonder if I should write her a letter and tell her I am all right."

"What are you going to write a letter with?" Phillip asked scornfully. "We haven't any paper or pens or ink. Think of all the money you'd squander buying all that."

"Perhaps the boatman has some."

Phillip laughed. "How often do you think a boatman writes a letter?"

"The lockmaster is bound to have some," Jeremy insisted. "He has to keep all kinds of records."

"And what makes you think he will let you use his supplies?"

"Nothing," said Jeremy. "But I am going to ask." He stood up and scrambled across the boats moored to the shore.

"You better be careful," Phillip warned. "If we get through the locks we aren't going to wait for you."

Jeremy grinned. "As slow as you'd be moving, I could catch you within minutes," he said as he climbed onto the bank and headed toward the lockmaster's house.

However, the lockmaster was busy supervising the numerous boats that were trying to pass through his domain and had no time to aid Jeremy in his quest. Dispirited, the lad finally climbed back into the boat.

"Maybe you can find something when we tie up tonight," Phillip said consolingly. The thought of writing a note to his papa never entered his head.

"I suppose," said Jeremy. Now that he was concerned about his mother, he did not like the delay.

Whyever had he not thought to leave a note when he left school, assuring her he would be all right and not to worry? That omission rankled him all afternoon as the narrow boat made its slow, tortuous way through Wiltshire.

"It is difficult to believe now the weather was so miserable," Emily said as she turned her face toward the warming sun. "'Tis warm as August today."

"And it will probably be raining again tomorrow," Hart said with a wry grin. He stretched out upon the blanket, which was littered with the remains of their picnic lunch.

"Then you must command it otherwise. Surely even the sun cannot resist a command from the Duke of Hartford."

"I doubt my power extends that far," Hart said. "After all, I cannot even find two runaway schoolboys with half the Runners of Bow Street at my beck and call."

Emily's mirthful expression sobered. "I cannot believe there has been no sign of them since Hitchin."

"I know." The duke looked thoughtful. "One would think they disappeared into thin air, except such a thing is not possible." He sighed. "I cannot bear the thought of returning to London without word, but I fear that remaining in Tring for days on end is of no use either."

"Is there any chance they did go with the fair folk, and they lied to the Runners?"

The duke shook his head. "I told my man to follow the fair, in case that was the situation. We would have found them by now if they were with them."

"And they have not been seen anywhere near the ports?"

"Nowhere. I cannot help but feel we have made an error in our thinking, but I will not even begin to guess where we went wrong. It seems fruitless to continue to look west when they have not been seen anywhere in the area."

Emily's hopeful expression wavered. "You are going to give up, then."

"No, I will not give up. But I begin to think that I need to send the men in a different direction." He looked at her for a moment, trying to lighten his expression. He did not wish to increase her apprehensions. "Did you read to your son any stories of Scottish fairies, Emily? Perhaps they have gone north. It is the only direction we have not searched thoroughly."

"But you remember what Robert Mayfield said. They were arguing about leprechauns."

"Perhaps Phillip persuaded Jeremy that they live to the north as well as in Ireland."

"Will you recall the men from Bristol and Liverpool, then?"

"No. It is still the best clue we have and I would be foolish to ignore it." He frowned. "Maybe I have miscalculated. We know they took the coach from New-market to Cambridge. But there is no reason to believe that they have been traveling by coach all the way. If they are on foot again, they will certainly be traveling at a much slower pace."

"You think we may be ahead of them?"

He shrugged. "They may be closer to us than we think. How far could those two walk in a day? Fifteen miles? Twenty? That takes us only a few hours in the carriage."

"Should we be looking back on the other side of the canal?"

"I wonder." The duke thought for a moment. "If we have not discovered anything by tomorrow, I will call back most of the Runners. They can return to Hitchin and work in every direction until we find some scrap of information."

Emily found Hart's discouragement infectious. Ever since he had taken over the search, he had imbued her with confidence that Jeremy would soon be found. But now, if even he began to doubt ... She turned a pleading look upon him. "Are we going to find them, Hart?"

"Yes," he said with a decisive air. "If for no other reason than I am itching to thoroughly thrash that young whelp for creating such a disorder in my life."

"I think I will be so relieved to see Jeremy again that I will not have the heart to thrash him," Emily declared. "Even though he certainly deserves it."

"I would be more than happy to take on that task," the duke said with a grin.

Emily laughed. "Trying to tell me how to raise my son again, your grace?"

"I merely do not want to see him indulged out of motherly squeamishness."

"I assure you, Hart, that I am capable of disciplining Jeremy when he needs it."

"I am certain you are."

Emily picked one of the small daisies that dotted the ground and twirled it in her fingers. "Still, I do sometimes wonder if I do limit Jeremy's life. It is so easy to deny him things with the excuse that we cannot afford them. A horse, for example. When deep down I am glad he cannot ride because it is one less thing to worry about."

"We can only protect our children so much," Hart said gently. "They have to learn to live in the world. We cannot always be there to help them."

"I wonder if that is what prompted this adventure," Emily said. "Did I put so many restraints on Jeremy that he felt the need for rebellion?"

"I do not know," the duke said with honesty. "But by the same token Phillip, who has been allowed a great deal of freedom, acted with your son. Perhaps we both went awry."

"Or our actions had no bearing whatsoever on this escapade." Emily smiled at her observation. "A more comforting thought, I find. It is certainly more soothing to my conscience, at least."

What Emily needed, Hart thought with sudden clarity, was more children. So that Jeremy was not the center of her universe. She would have less time to worry and fret over his behavior if she had a half-dozen boys and girls to occupy her time. He could almost imagine a little girl sitting next to her, clutching a fold of Emily's skirt in her chubby little fingers.

And with a burning shock of realization, he more vividly visualized the process of creating those children. Emily, her slight form dwarfed by the massive bed at Stratton, her dark, curling locks spread out over the crisp white linen of the pillow slip. Hart pictured her smiling face beneath his as he slid into the hot warmth of her body . . .

What would it be like to make love to her? She presented a facade of peaceful calm, but he had felt the sharp edge of her tongue enough to know that there was a layer of passion beneath that prim exterior. Would she release that passion further in bed? Had Stephen seen that also, and was it that which had attracted his old friend to this rather unassuming woman?

Hart watched Emily with narrowed eyes, admiring the measured rise and fall of her trim bosom. Although voluptuous was not the word to describe her shape, she certainly had enough curves to spark his interest. He did not mind at all that her austerely tailored spencer was a trifle too tight. The slight breeze blew untidy wisps of hair about her face, softening her look and bringing a hint of color to the cheeks that had been far too pale from strain. She was not a beautiful woman, but had an unpolished prettiness that was as unaffected as it was refreshing.

As he felt his groin tighten, Hart took a deep breath. This was an exercise in foolishness. Was he such a weak spirit that he could not be away from a woman for a week without reacting like a silly schoolboy to every female he saw?

Yet there was nothing wrong with his admiring Emily. She did have a certain alluring quality about her. Dressed in better clothes, with her hair arranged in a fashionable style, she would turn more than a few heads in town. But the thought of a sexual relationship with her was ridiculous. She would never allow it. He knew instinctively that she was not the type of widow who would take a lover—and that was the only type of widow who appealed to him. There were far too many women eager for his attentions to bother with one who was not.

Besides, all his energy should be focused on finding Phillip. That was the important thing. Yet he could not help but wonder exactly how Emily would feel as he covered her body with his. Hart laughed aloud at his weakness.

Emily turned to look at him. "What is it that you find so amusing?"

"I was merely contemplating the baser nature of man," he said, unable to keep a wicked grin from his face.

"A highly entertaining topic," she admitted. "One on which you are no doubt an expert."

"No doubt."

Emily was tempted to wipe the smug expression from his face with an icy retort, but something in his eyes stopped her. Accustomed to seeing the ice in them, she was surprised at the unexpected warmth they now held. That must be what tropical seas looked like, she thought, soft and blue and warm.

And with a sudden shock, she realized that if the duke had been entertaining base thoughts, they were most likely about her. There was blatant admiration and invitation in those eyes. She looked away in quick confusion.

Take a deep breath, she told herself firmly. It was

only her imagination carrying her into wild flights of
fancy. A man with a reputation like the Duke of Hartford's would have no interest in such a plain creature
as her. She could only guess how she must suffer in
comparison with all the elegant ladies in London. He
was most likely reminiscing about his latest mistress.
Or that barmaid in Royston.

Still, just the mere thought that he might have been
looking at *her* like that sent chills up her spine. It was
a very different sensation from the one provoked by
her odious brother-in-law when he laid his hands on
her at every opportunity. Emily stole a hasty glance at
the duke's long, slim fingers. Would they cause the
same disturbing sensation if they trailed up her arm?
Or would it remind her of Stephen, whose lightest
touch had sent her into the heavens? Or would Hart's
touch be totally unlike anything she had ever experienced or imagined? For a brief moment she desperately wanted to know.

Emily shook her head, chiding herself for her
fanciful thoughts. What would the Duke of Hartford
want with a dowdy, countrified widow? They had
nothing in common except their two wayward sons.
The duke had no desire to touch her—nor did she wish
him to. Not at all.

"We should return to the inn," Hart said abruptly.
"We have been away long enough. News may have arrived."

"True," said Emily, brushing the shredded flower
petals off her skirt.

The duke stood with agile grace, extending his hand
to Emily. She clasped it firmly, then nearly lost her
grip as she recoiled from the intense warmth of his
palm, improper thoughts flooding her mind. Quickly,
she clambered to her feet and snatched back her hand.
In the carriage, she took great care to make certain
there was a great deal of space between them. Fanciful
imaginings or not, she was suddenly very aware of the

man who sat beside her. Achingly aware of him as a man.

"I enjoyed the afternoon," the duke said, as he guided the horses back to the lane. "We have been traveling so quickly this last week I have not had time to appreciate the country."

"Do you spend a great deal of time at your estate?" Emily asked, relieved to have a safe topic of discussion.

"No," he said. "I fall prey to the temptations of London and do not go home as often as I would like. And Phillip, of course, prefers the delights of the city, so I often find myself there even in the summer."

"I missed it at first, when I retired to Lincolnshire. But now I do not know if I would ever wish to live there for any length of time. There is a peace in the country that cannot be found elsewhere."

"Yet as soon as I find it, I grow restless for the life of the city," the duke said.

"You are a difficult man to please."

The duke grinned. "You are not the first to say that."

"A sentiment expressed by your numerous mistresses, no doubt," Emily blurted, then felt the color rise in her cheeks. Why had she said such a thing?

His grin widened. "They, among others. But come, Emily, you do not strike me as a woman who is easy to please either. Do you condemn me for a fault which you share?"

"I have learned that life is easier when you are content with your situation, whatever it is," she said.

"But does that not leave you without ambition, or a desire to change your life?"

"When there is little hope for change, it is foolish to wish for it," she said quietly. She cast him a sidelong glance. "And change for the sake of change is not always welcome. There is a measure of security in sameness."

"And a lack of adventure. Do you not have dreams, Emily?"

"I dream of a new roof for the hall and a bountiful harvest," she said. "They are simple dreams, perhaps, but heartfelt ones."

"The words of a landowner," Hart chided gently. "Have you no plans for yourself, Emily?"

"Right now, my greatest wish is finding Jeremy."

"And Phillip." The duke sighed. "It is difficult to imagine how two young boys can cause such havoc. Perhaps I shall put Phillip into the dungeon for a year or two after this escapade."

"You have a dungeon at Stratton?"

"No. But right now I wish I did."

"Parenthood is not always the easiest job," Emily admitted.

"Particularly for a lone woman," the duke added with a pointed glance at his companion. He reached out and patted her hand. "I want you to know that I am willing to offer you my help whenever you should request it."

Emily looked at him with wary suspicion. "Because you think I need it?"

"No. Because I would like to give it. I think my friendship with Stephen allows me that privilege."

Emily hesitated. She did not think the duke was motivated purely by altruism. But what could he possibly hope to gain by helping her?

Unless she had not misinterpreted that glance at the stream side. The thought sent a frisson of apprehension and—anticipation?—up her spine. For however much she wished to deny it, the duke had awakened a part of her that had long been dead. She did not know whether to despair or be grateful.

The thought of the duke having a part in her life—however small—after the boys were found did not sit easily upon her mind. He would only want to take over and manage things in his own way. What could he hope to accomplish by it? No, it was better that they both returned to their own lives when the search was over. However much she might need it, she did not want his or anyone else's help. She managed well enough.

Emily chose to ignore the tiny voice inside her head that spoke of the advantages that could come of the duke's friendship. Advantages for Jeremy, of course. A male presence in his life. Entry into the circles to which the duke belonged, when Jeremy grew old enough to participate.

No. She shook her head sadly. She would go on as she always had—alone. Jeremy would be none the worse for it. And she knew it was best for her. Simply because she wanted to accept Hart's help—so that she could continue to see him. Which was a foolish reason.

It was all the fault of this crazy adventure. She felt freer now than she had in years, and the giddy sense of freedom was clouding her judgment. Emily firmly reminded herself that this was only a temporary respite from her real life, and she would be back to it soon enough. It was foolish to spin daydreams about a different future. Emily knew exactly what her future was to be. And the Duke of Hartford did not play a part in it.

11

Emily, her emotions still in a tangle, managed to hide her disquiet during dinner. She consented to play a few indifferent hands of cards, but made her excuses as early as she dared and fled gratefully to her room.

She could not help but be suspicious of Hart. He had criticized her for days now, yet suddenly he was all smiles and friendliness. Was he using this new tactic to convince her of the correctness of his ideas? Was it only a more clever attempt to convince her of the error of her ways?

Or did the duke sincerely want to help? He had mentioned Stephen as a reason.

Perhaps it all came down to what type of help the duke meant. She would not accept any financial assistance—her fierce pride forbade that. But were there areas where the duke's help could be gladly accepted? Or would there be unnamed strings attached to his offer—strings in which she did not want to become entangled?

There was no denying it would be wonderful to lay aside her burdens and shift her responsibilities onto strong male shoulders. What joy to allow someone else to worry about the state of this year's crops, or whence the funding would come to fix the roof or buy Jeremy a new pair of shoes. For just a moment, the temptation to succumb to the duke's help was strong, but Emily shook her head in denial. She had not managed alone for so long now to be trapped by a moment of weakness.

It was worry over Jeremy that made her so susceptible to the duke's offer. She had resisted offers from all her family in the past because she knew that with the help would come control. Ultimately, the duke would prove no different.

She would accept his help in the matter of finding Jeremy because their goals in this case coincided. But when the boys were found and safely installed back at school, she and the duke would go their separate ways. Emily valued her life; she had worked hard to gain the degree of independence she enjoyed, and she was not going to let anyone influence the course she had chosen for herself. Not even a man as compelling as the duke.

Emily awoke in the morning refreshed and determined to resist any more temptations. The sun shone brightly and the day looked full of possibilities. If only they could find some word of the boys.

The duke had already breakfasted before she came down and was busily engaged in his correspondence. Emily nibbled at her meal. "What is your plan for today?" she asked when the breakfast dishes had been removed.

The duke looked up from his writing. "We will be returning to Hitchin as soon as I make the arrangements. The trail there may be old, but it is the best we have."

Emily knew it was an admission of defeat—however temporarily—and she strove to remain cheerful. "You will not be particularly welcome at the inn, you know."

The duke smiled ruefully. "Let us hope, then, that we shall not be forced to remain there for any length of time."

"Are you contacting the Runners?" Emily looked at the growing pile of letters.

"Them and others," Hart replied. "I am having my traveling carriage sent up from London. For your comfort."

"That is not necessary."

"I insist. There is no need to expose you to any more drenchings. And inclement weather will no longer discourage us from acting."

Emily realized he was doing this more for her benefit than his and she felt a mixture of gratitude and guilt. Would he have searched more ruthlessly if she had not been with him? "Perhaps I should return home."

The duke gave her a searching stare. "Do you wish to do so?"

Emily thought about Mrs. Harris tending the herb garden alone. About the hay cutting that should be started soon. All the things that needed to be done at Longridge. All the things she wanted to continue to forget for a time. "No," she confessed.

"Then do not." The duke returned to his letter.

Emily's heart filled with gladness. He did not wish her gone. He was not going to cut their adventure short. For a while longer—as long as it took to find the boys—she could still be free. Free to be herself, without responsibilities to hem her in. Free to enjoy the duke's company. Free of everything—except worry over Jeremy.

Satisfied with Emily's choice, the duke sealed the letters he had written. He would not have argued if she had decided otherwise, but he was glad she would be with him still. It would make the search more pleasant. By tomorrow, at the latest, the Runners would be scouring the nearby countryside. Somebody had to have seen those rascals.

Hart glanced at Emily, who sat near the window in her usual state of composure. He wished there was some way he could give her some money, to ease her worries on that head. The search was taking longer than either of them had expected. He would pare the monies she owed him to the bone, but he knew she would insist on repaying him for her expenses. It was her damn independent pride. She needed to learn when it was beneficial to rely on another. Accepting aid from him did not mean she was compromising any of her principles. But he knew he would not be able to persuade her of that—at least not without another week of alternately arguing and cajoling. But he needed to spend his time looking for their sons.

Still, there were ways a few things could be managed. He would send a man on into Lincolnshire to investigate the situation. There must be ways to add monies to the estate coffers without Emily being the wiser. Somehow, he would find a way to assist her, whether she wanted him to or not.

Perhaps her son could come home with Phillip during the summer break. Hart could give him a glimpse of life outside of his isolated estate in Lincolnshire, and introduce him to the society to which he would belong when he became of age. Lady Darrow would not be so foolish as to begrudge her son the opportunity of such an advantageous visit. And in the process, he could make a start at directing a more masculine influence on young Darrow.

A week of knocking around London and Stratton would give the lad a glimpse of real life. Hart would take the boys to the races or a mill. Jeremy deserved to have the same chances as Phillip. Stephen would want it.

Hart chose to ignore what he knew would be Emily's objections. When he found Jeremy for her, none the worse for his adventure, she would be more willing to admit that Hart was right about her overprotectiveness.

The duke smiled smugly as he pressed his signet ring into the last blob of sealing wax. He would not be able to undo all of her detrimental influences in such a short time, he knew, but he would do what he could.

* * *

Emily edged her chair closer to the window to take advantage of the morning light. Not that she was absorbed in her sewing, but the duke was still busy making arrangements for their departure. Now that the decision was made, she was eager to be off again.

They had only been traveling together for a week, but it seemed a much longer time. Yet when she thought how little she knew about him, it seemed remarkable they had been together even that long. She did not know his favorite foods, if he enjoyed music or the opera, the type of clothes he normally wore, or even the type of women he liked—

Her mind rebelled at that last thought. That was a characteristic she could probably supply. Willing women. Who were probably not in short supply for a duke with his force of personality and depth of pocket. He was not truly handsome, but the confidence and power he exuded more than made up for that. He would draw women to him like bees to honey, a fact of which he was quite aware. He knew it well. It could be seen in the way he dealt with women—joking and teasing with the landlady, shamelessly flirting with the young barmaids they encountered. In short, the way he treated every woman but herself.

Emily could no longer deny the attraction she felt for him, puzzling as it was. There were many things about him that she truly disliked. Yet that did not lessen her interest. It was as if she were two persons— the fiercely independent widow who resented a domineering male, and a deeply sensual woman who saw a potential lover in the rakish duke.

Emily lifted her eyes to the ceiling. Where were these wayward thoughts coming from? It was as if the duke's lusty nature was leaking out and infecting her with its strength. Here she was, desiring a man she was not wholly certain she liked. It was not like her at all. Emily thought desire had died within her at the death of her husband. Why did it reemerge now—and with Hartford, of all people? Something surely was wrong with her thinking.

It *was* time to resume the search. The Duke of Hartford was starting to be a very bad influence upon her. They had to find the boys soon. Or else she might find herself willing to compromise all her principles under his seductive and beguiling ways.

A short, wiry man entered the room, and Hart set down his pen. "Two young boys were spotted at Abingdon on Thursday. Boarding one of the coal boats."

The duke jumped to his feet, scattering papers across the table. "Tell me more."

"They were heading westward, your grace. The coal boats go back to the mines empty most times. One of the boatmen took up the two as passengers."

"Any description of the two lads?"

The man shook his head. "Just a report that two young boys were taken aboard."

"What canal is that?"

"The Wilts-and-Berks, yer grace."

Hart frowned. "Where does that lead?"

"Through the Vale of the White Horse, past Swindon, then down to join the Kennet-and-Avon," the man explained.

"Bath!" the duke exclaimed.

"Aye, the Kennet-and-Avon leads there."

"And Bristol is just beyond! Emily! Be ready to go in an instant." The duke dashed out the door.

Emily was on her feet immediately, brushing past the Runner and racing to the stairs. She hastily packed her bag, all the time praying that this was the clue they had been looking for. Oh, please, please, she prayed, let it be them. And let us catch them this time.

When she finished, she crossed the hall to Hart's room, knowing he would value every minute saved.

Emily could pack his things while he had the carriage readied. That would please him.

The sight that met her eyes in Hart's room appalled her. Clothes were strewn about the room in a haphazard fashion. A jacket lay draped over the arm of a chair; a shirt dangled across the seat, its sleeve brushing the floor.

What a picture of chaos! It was obvious that although the duke traveled without his valet, he certainly was not doing the work of one. Fortunately, his portmanteau sat on the chair by his bed. Emily grabbed at the clothes that lay scattered about the room, folding them into a hasty semblance of neatness as she crammed them into the bag.

"What the devil?" The duke stood at the door, looking at Emily in puzzlement.

"I thought to speed our departure by packing for you," Emily explained.

"Oh." Hart crossed the room and gathered up his shaving items atop the dresser. Placing them in the bag, he quickly scanned the chamber, noting that everything had been collected. He shut the bag with a definitive motion and fastened the straps. Carrying it into the hall, he picked up Emily's portmanteau and headed down the stairs.

"Is the Runner going with us?" she asked.

Hart shook his head as he handed Emily into the carriage. "He is to stay here in case there is other news, then relay it to Abingdon."

"Is it a great distance from here?"

"It is not close, I am afraid," he said as he sprang aboard and took the reins. With a quick flick he urged the horses out into the lane that comprised the main street of Tring. "We are going to take a rather roundabout way, but I think we will make quicker time on the main roads than if we strike out across the country. So we will go to Aylesbury."

"It appears they are on their way to Bristol after all,"

Emily mused aloud as she grabbed the side of the carriage to regain her balance.

"I think you are right." Hart whipped the horses into a spanking trot as they reached the open road. "And I intend that we get there first."

"But they are days ahead of us."

"Canal boats do not travel swiftly," he explained. "And according to the Runner, this particular canal is full of locks that will slow their progress. As long as we have no mishaps on the road, we should be able to catch them at last."

The trip to Aylesbury reminded Emily of their frantic dash on the first day of travel, when the duke had sped to Newmarket and then to Cambridge. They reached Aylesbury in less than an hour. Hart stopped only long enough to change horses; then they raced out of town, toward Oxford.

Emily's nerves were stretched taut by the time they reached the university town. Hart reluctantly halted there for a late lunch. They had made only the briefest of stops since leaving Tring and she was grateful for the chance to be free of the bouncing curricle even for a short while.

The town clock was chiming four when the carriage raced through Abingdon toward the canal basin alongside the Thames.

"We shall see now if more has been learned," Hart said when he pulled up in front of the lockmaster's building.

Emily followed him into the room, fear clutching at her heart. What if it was all a false alarm? That the boys seen were not Jeremy and Phillip at all? Or, almost worse, what if there was no new information and that slight clue was all the information they had? Would Hart feel it enough to justify traveling all the way to Bristol?

She sought to calm her racing pulse. Whatever Hart thought about making the journey to Bristol, it did not matter. Someone was already there looking for the boys. The important thing was trying to discover if it really had been Jeremy and Phillip who boarded that canal boat three days ago. It would be an assurance that they were still safe.

"I can't remember much," the lockmaster was saying in response to Hart's barrage of questions. "They hitched a ride with Old Billy, they did, I knows that much."

"Try to remember what they looked like," Hart said. "It is important."

"Can't," said the man. "Just lads they were. Nothing special."

"Was one perhaps red-haired, with freckles?" Emily asked.

The man thought. "I don't think so. One was blond, mebbe, t'other dark."

Hart's face lit with a triumphant smile. It had to be them. "How long will it take them to reach the end of the canal?"

"Depends on the lockages and how long they travel each day. Takes a good three-four days to reach the end of the Wilts-and-Berks."

"Then it is likely they have not even reached the junction with the Kennet-and-Avon yet?" Hart asked hopefully.

"They could be getting close," the lockman said. "Old Bill ain't one to dally seeings how there's a cargo to come back this way when he reaches the coal barges. But traffic's been heavy and that means a slow-down at the locks waitin' for all the east-bound boats."

"You've been a great help," Hart said, throwing down some coins upon the table. He took Emily's elbow and led her back to the carriage.

He stopped beside the horses and gave her a searching look. "This will be a mad dash," he said with a warning look. "Do you still wish to go on?"

"I cannot stay behind, Hart," she said. "Not if I can find Jeremy."

"I am going to head south toward the Bath road," he explained as he whipped up the horses. "T'will get us there faster. The country roads that follow the canal are not made for rapid travel."

"Will we reach Bath this evening?" Emily asked.

Hart shook his head. "We shall be lucky to reach Marlborough tonight," he said. "Thank God the weather has cleared. I would not relish making this journey in the rain."

"Will anyone be looking for them along the canal?" she asked. "What if they decided to leave the boat and travel on foot again?"

"One of the Runners left for Bath yesterday," Hart said. "He will work eastward up the canal, looking for them."

"It is possible he might even find them before we do." Emily could not keep the excitement out of her voice.

"Very possible," Hart said. "In which case we can end this blasted journey in Bath without having to go to Bristol. But we will leave nothing to chance. The net is closing in on them, and I do not intend for them to slip out of it this time."

Emily sat back against the seat, tears of relief springing to her eyes. It had seemed like an age since the first horrendous news of Jeremy's disappearance jolted her out of her simple existence. Now it looked as if they would find him by tomorrow. She could not wait.

Once again Hart drove quickly and steadily, stopping only to change horses. They ate a quick dinner in Newbury, then sped down the Bath road toward Marlborough. The lengthy June nights worked to their advantage, although the light was growing dim by the time Hart pulled up in front of the Castle Inn.

"I do not like staying at the coaching inns," he said, "but when speed is critical, it is the best. They are accustomed to having their clients depart in haste in the morning. And I wish to be gone at first light."

"I will be ready," Emily said as she stifled a yawn. Sleep would not be a worrisome problem for her tonight.

Indeed, it seemed as though her head had only touched the pillow when the serving maid came to wake her in the pre-dawn light. Emily ate a slice of bread and sipped her tea while she dressed in the early-morning chill.

"You are punctual as usual, Emily," Hart said when she met him downstairs.

"I am eager to see Jeremy. Oh, Hart, do you think we will find them today?"

"I make no promises, but if we do not, I think we shall be very close. We will know when we reach Semington, which is where the two canals meet. If they have passed through that junction, we will nab them easily."

For Emily, the trip to Bath passed by in a blur of road traffic, hasty changes of horses, and the unrolling scenery of the passing countryside. They left the main road only once, at Semington, to inquire whether Old Bill had brought his boat through yet. No one was quite certain if he had or hadn't. Or whether he was traveling all the way to the junction with the Somerset Coal Canal, or whether he was planning to wait in Semington to load his coal from the larger boats that plied the Kennet-and-Avon.

Hart's face was a picture of frustration when he returned to the carriage. "Nothing," he said to Emily as he took up the reins.

"Should we stay here and wait, do you think?"

The duke considered. "No," he said at last. "Let's drive on to Bath. We can eat, and decide which course we want to take. I have plenty of men here to grab them if they have yet to come through. But if they are ahead of us, I think we need to keep on toward Bristol."

Emily could hardly contain her excitement. With Hart's men scattered about the countryside, it might only be a matter of hours before the boys were found. They would not reach Bristol without being discovered. It looked as if she would be with her son again, very, very soon.

And she owed it all to Hart. A growing warmth spread through her at the thought. She honestly did not know how she could have managed if she had been forced to face this on her own. All along, she had drawn on his strength to quell her fears. Thank God he had the fortitude she needed.

If only she could rely on him in the future as well. But sadly, Emily knew that was not to be. She must remain grateful for what she had now, and not repine for the impossible.

12

Despite no news of the boys in Bath, Emily's conviction that she would soon be reunited with Jeremy did not waver as the duke guided the carriage toward Bristol. She could not help but expect that they would find the two in the port city, held securely by the duke's men.

Hart was forced to ask directions more than once as the horses wended their way through Bristol's jumble of streets. At last, he pulled up in front of an ancient timbered building whose sign proclaimed it to be the Hatchet Inn.

"We are not going to the docks first?" Emily asked in some confusion.

"*I* am going to the docks. You will remain here."

Emily opened her mouth to protest, but he cut her off firmly.

"The Bristol docks are no place for a lady," he said. "I can accomplish more there without having to worry about you."

Emily took a deep breath and counted to ten. Losing her temper would serve no purpose now. Speed was of the utmost importance, and if Hart could find the boys quicker by her remaining here, she would.

Without waiting for him to climb down, she jumped from the carriage and stalked into the inn. Hart followed.

"You will be more comfortable here," he assured her

as the innkeeper ushered them into a private dining parlor.

"Most certainly," Emily replied with a tinge of sarcasm. Searching for Jeremy, not sitting in a comfortable inn, would have been her own choice.

The duke hastily made arrangements with the landlord, then turned to Emily. "I will send word the moment I learn anything," he said reassuringly. "It cannot take long to check with the packet boats."

"And what if they have slipped aboard some cargo vessel?" she asked. "We will never find them."

"More Runners will be here later today," he explained. "We will scour every dock. And I will send men on to Ireland if I have the slightest inkling that they may have already departed."

Emily bowed her head in acquiescence. She knew Hart would do all that he could. It was the waiting, alone, that was so difficult.

"Try to rest," he said gently. "It has been an exhausting two days of travel. You will feel the better for it later."

Rest was the last thing Emily could imagine as she paced up and down the floor of the tiny room. But when the landlady bustled in with a food-laden tray, Emily surprised herself by eating a large luncheon. In the drowsy contentment that followed, she was forced to admit that the thought of a short nap did sound appealing. Upon being escorted to the room bespoken for her by Hart, Emily lay down upon the bed, determined only to rest her eyes for a little while.

While he waited for Emily to awaken, Hart sat in a comfortable chair, savoring the delicious claret brought to him by the landlady. For an ancient, out-of-the-way inn, the comfort here was an unexpected surprise.

He hoped Emily did not mind the subterfuge he had employed, but the arrangement of these particular rooms had been too convenient to ignore. Having a private sitting room afforded them a degree of privacy that justified the lie. Besides, once those rascals were found, they would be out of Bristol in an instant.

He was glad Emily was resting. He knew that his news—or rather, the lack of it—would be upsetting. He was not totally surprised that there was no sign of the boys at the docks. He was convinced he and Emily were ahead of them at last, and would only have to wait for those miscreants to wander into town. But would Emily view the matter as calmly? She had shown an amazing amount of fortitude on this trip, but the rising expectations and the frantic pace of the last two days had been a strain on both of them.

Emily was a remarkable woman. He laughed wryly at his initial reluctance to take her along while he searched for the boys. He had thought she would be an annoying inconvenience. Instead, she had proved to be an undemanding companion. A bit exasperating at times, but certainly he had never seriously thought of leaving her behind after that first day. She was pluck to the backbone. Not the usual attribute he admired in a woman, but he could not help but admire Emily.

He wondered what she had been like all those years ago, when she first made her bow in society and bowled Stephen over with her winsome ways. Would he have even given her a moment's notice? He had never paid much attention to the crop of giggling females who made their debuts each spring in London; the understanding with Louisa meant he had no need to seek out a wife from the crop of hopefuls. Oh, he had done the pretty on a few occasions at the glittering come-out balls, but even then he was looking for less-demanding prey. In fact, he had spent the months before his marriage in an excess of sexual adventures, reasoning that he needed to enjoy himself before he become a settled married fellow.

That had been a laugh. He would certainly have scandalized all of society with his behavior if Louisa had not been so obliging as to die in childbirth. Discretion had not been a part of his makeup then, even if he had learned it over the years. Thank God no one paid any attention to the behavior of a bachelor.

He was content with that life. Moving from one lady to another as his fancy struck him. There were some who had held his interest for long periods of time, others with whom he parted after only the briefest of liaisons.

Yet he was gradually developing the sense that something was missing from his life. Which was a laughable thought. He had everything. Money, position, power. A son—however much a rascal he was— who would inherit it all when his sire was dead. His money could buy him anything he wished. If Hart was finding that he wanted less and less, well, it was because he had everything he needed.

So why was there this growing dissatisfaction? The feeling that for all his wealth and power, his stable full of racing horses, his magnificent estate and his enticing mistress, he did not have a perfect life?

He snorted his derision. What a callous soul he had become. Emily struggled and scrimped and saved just to survive and hang on to a tiny estate, so she could pass it on to her son. He was an ungrateful bastard to think that there was something wrong with his life when he compared it to hers. She had cause for complaint. He did not.

Hart was still determined to do what he could to ease Emily's situation. There were all sorts of creative ways he could apply his wealth to aid her, without Emily being any bit the wiser.

Perhaps that was what he needed—something useful to do. Taking care of Emily would fill that need. Hart's expression turned calculating. He would have his man of business look into matters as soon as he returned to London. Some careful sleight-of-hand could be employed to pump money into the estate coffers.

It would be a mighty challenge to help Emily without arousing her suspicions. But Hart liked challenges. He wished he could help her personally, furnishing her with a new wardrobe, one that was stylish and elegant, with the bright hues that would suit her. She would look lovely in a deep green or a brilliant amethyst.

Reluctantly, he shook his head. He could only help her as long as she did not realize he was doing so. Short of setting fire to every gown she owned, he could not think of any manner of argument that would convince her to accept a single item of clothing from him.

But he wanted to help her so badly. It would enable him to think about someone else besides himself for a change. Not that he was selfish. But except for Phillip, he did not have anyone else to think about. Perhaps it was a part of human nature to want to look out for and protect those of the weaker sex.

Emily guided the curricle in hot pursuit of the carriage in front. She knew Jeremy was inside. The road twisted and curved and she could only catch fleeting glimpses of the racing carriage. Faster, she urged the horses, but they could gain no ground. The curricle careened around a sharp corner. At the sight of the overturned chaise, Emily frantically sawed at the reins, jerking her own vehicle to a halt. She jumped to the ground and raced to the carriage. Pulling and tugging on the door, she cried aloud in despair when it would not open. She pulled again, the door popped free, and she—

Emily woke with a start, her heart pounding. She looked about the unfamiliar room in confusion. Bristol, she remembered. She was at the inn.

Dear God, it had only been a dream.

The room lay in darkened shadow. Emily scrambled into her clothes and dashed into the hall, frantic to find

Hart. She nearly overset the landlady, who stood outside the door with an enormous tray in her arms.

"Glad to see you are awake, Mrs. Elliott," the landlady greeted. "Your husband is waiting in the parlor." She nodded at the next door in the passage.

Emily stared in confusion at the landlady, her sleep-befuddled mind unable to understand the words. "My husband?"

The landlady shook her head sympathetically as she pushed the door open for Emily. "He told me what you have been through, chasing all over the countryside after those two lads of yours. All will be well soon, I am certain of it."

Emily peered over the landlady's shoulder. Hart sat at the table in the middle of the room.

"Ah, there you are, my dear," he said, getting to his feet. "Did you rest well?"

"Have you found them?" Emily asked anxiously.

He shook his head, then darted to her side in alarm at the sight of Emily's whitened face. He guided her to a chair. "No passenger boats have left for Ireland for several days. They could not possibly be that far ahead of us. They are still in England."

"Might they have found passage on some other boat?"

"No one I spoke with recalls seeing two young boys hanging about the docks. Two of the Runners arrived late this afternoon, and they are nosing about." He clasped her hand in a comforting gesture. "I honestly think we can say we have outwitted them at last. Thanks to your penchant for leprechauns."

Emily put her free hand to her forehead. "I had the most dreadful dream . . ." She looked at him with curiosity. "What is this taradiddle you have told the innkeeper about your 'wife'?"

Hart looked abashed. "She naturally assumed . . . and I did nothing to disabuse her of the notion." He made a sweeping gesture with his arm. "As a result, we have this lovely parlor with adjoining rooms. It will afford us more privacy."

Emily nodded absently. Her life had been turned so upside-down over the last fortnight that the sudden acquisition of a husband did not seem out of the ordinary at all.

"Are you ready to eat?" he asked. "I waited for you."

"I had an enormous lunch," Emily explained, "but please do eat if you are hungry."

Hart summoned the landlady again. In a very short time, a vast array of food was set before them.

While Hart tore into his meal with his usual relish, Emily contented herself with a small portion of new spring peas.

"The chicken is quite good," Hart told her. "Do try some. You have eaten so little."

"I really have no appetite," she confessed. "I was so certain that . . . that Jeremy would be here. Which is foolish, I know," she said with a dismissive wave of her hand. "But ever since we left Abingdon I had an image of pulling up in front of the dock and seeing him there and . . ." Her voice quavered.

"Imagine instead the look on their faces when they arrive at the docks to find us waiting for them," Hart rejoined. "I wager there will be no more surprised boys in the whole of England."

Emily laughed lightly. It was a much more pleasing picture.

"Now eat," he commanded. "Before I feed you myself."

Emily offered him a meek smile and took a bite of chicken.

Later, when the dishes had been taken away, they sat before the cold fire grate on a worn but comfortably upholstered settee.

"You still look tired," Hart said suddenly, setting

down his empty glass on the side table. "You need not remain here if you should like to retire."

Emily laid a staying hand on his arm. "Not yet," she said with a gently pleading look. "I should like to sit awhile. I slept the entire afternoon."

"Would you care for more claret?"

"I think not," Emily said, already feeling the effects of the wine. "It is a treat with which I am too little accustomed."

"Then you should enjoy it," he said, refilling both their glasses. He sat again, his long legs stretched out before him, content with the peaceful silence.

The absence of conversation allowed Emily's thoughts to dwell on her son, and the longer she thought, the more concerned she grew. They were relying so much on her firm conviction that the boys were headed across the Irish Sea. But could that really be the reason for the boys' flight?

"What if I have been wrong about Ireland?" Emily blurted out. "The boys have not been seen since they boarded the canal boat at Abingdon. What if they are not making for Ireland at all?"

"As you pointed out to me previously, we heard what Robert Mayfield said—they were arguing about leprechauns."

"But that may have been all it was—a silly argument. This whole journey could have some other purpose. One that is not going to bring them to Bristol."

"They have been heading steadily in this direction since they left school." Hart countered, amused that they should suddenly be reversing sides.

"But Abingdon is so far away," Emily insisted, the panic rising in her voice. "So many things could have happened. . . . Even on the canal. Jeremy does not know how to swim, you know."

"Emily, you must believe they are safe."

"I cannot," she said, her voice breaking in a sob as she lost the power to withhold her tears. She had been living on hope and anticipation for so many days, yet it suddenly seemed that she no longer had the strength for either. All the dire fears she had first imagined when she learned of Jeremy's absence came rushing back over her. Jeremy, her only child, lying injured—or worse—at the bottom of a ditch. The image of the smashed carriage in her dream reappeared and her self-control crumbled.

Hart clasped her hands in his. "Emily, you know they are safe," he insisted. "We would know if something had happened."

"Jeremy is so young," she said between her sobs. "And he is all I have."

Hart reached out and pulled Emily into his arms. "It is all right to cry," he said as he stroked her hair.

Emily buried her face against his chest and succumbed to her fear and despair.

Hart held her tightly, murmuring soothing words, knowing she needed this moment of release. When her sobs became sniffles, and her shoulders ceased to shake, he withdrew one encircling arm and drew out his handkerchief.

Emily took the pristine white cloth, embarrassed that she had so lost her composure in front of him. "I am sorry," she apologized as she dabbed at her eyes. "I know I am being foolish."

"You are not a bit foolish," Hart said. "You are only a mother who is worried sick about her son. Good God, Emily, you have been through hell in the last week. I think a few tears are understandable."

Emily looked at him, seeing the concern and care in his eyes. He was so full of confidence. What had once seemed arrogance now seemed strength. How she wished she could draw some of that from him right now. She needed his strength, needed his arms wrapped around her, holding her, comforting her, while he made the bad dream go away. Oh, God, how she needed him. Just for a while.

Emily knew she should move, but she was reluctant to leave the comfort of Hart's arms. Only a few moments longer, she promised herself. Only a few more moments of pretending he was holding her out of more than mere kindness.

She laid her head against his shoulder. She felt so secure in his arms. Secure and . . . desirable. She realized that what she wanted most from him was not consolation or sympathy, but simply him. She wanted his acknowledgment that she was a woman, with a woman's needs and desires. Only for a little while. For now.

Hart felt the tenseness leave her body as she nestled against him. She was warm and soft. Very womanly. Very desirable. The desire that had been creeping up on him slowly was fanned into flames by her nearness. Emily felt entirely too nice in his arms. The faint scent of her perfume tantalized him.

Hart was perplexed. He had never once wanted a woman he could not have, or felt that he should not want. But with Emily . . . He was dangerously close to throwing his scruples aside.

And although his mind might have been firmly convinced of the unsuitability of any action, his body was not listening. As Emily relaxed, he tensed as growing desire flooded through him.

Hart's arms tightened around her and he brushed the top of her head with his lips. A chaste action, he reassured himself. He instantly regretted the impulse when Emily lifted her head from his shoulder.

He expected to see condemnation in her eyes. Instead he saw warm invitation in their depths.

Hart hesitatingly ran a hand down her arm, capturing her fingers in his. "Emily?" Her eyes answered his question.

Hart dipped his head and touched his lips to hers for a brief instant. Then he kissed her again, confident, eager, hungry. To his great delight, she responded as he hoped she would.

Emily knew this was folly. But she did not care. She pushed thoughts of all but Hart from her mind. She wanted him as he wanted her, and she would not turn back from what had been started. For once she was going to think only of herself. His kisses grew more heated and she responded with eagerness.

"Emily," Hart groaned, his lips trailing kisses across her cheek. "Send me away now."

"Why?"

He drew back and looked at her with a fond smile. "If you know what is good for you, Emily, you will bolt for your room and bar the door."

"And if I do not?"

"Then," he said as he drew her to him again, "you must accept the consequences."

He kissed her again with an intensity that left her breathless—and wanting more. "Stay with me," she said. "I do not wish to be alone tonight."

Hart eyed her steadily, his gaze unwavering. Reaching out, he gently stroked his fingers along her cheek. "Are you so very certain, Emily?"

"Yes," she replied.

"I should like that, Emily. Very much." His eyes gleamed with anticipation while his hands moved in soothing patterns along her back. "It will be wonderful," he whispered in her ear before he kissed her with the full force of his desire.

Emily was not certain how long they lingered in the sitting room. Their kisses and embraces grew more and more heated, and she lost all ability to think or reason. When they at last moved to the bedroom, Hart undressed her carefully, reverently, as if handling a rare and priceless treasure.

"You are so beautiful," he said as he undid the top ribbon of her chemise.

She felt an uneasy delight in his intent gaze, and laughed lightly. "Hardly. You need not dress things up in seductive words, Hart."

"Do not undervalue yourself, Emily" he said as he traced the line of her collarbone with his lips.

His touch sent shivers of newly reawakened desire through her. Surprised by her eagerness, Emily tugged at his shirt, freeing it from the waistband of his breeches. She ran a hand across his chest, reveling in the feel of the crisp blond curls that covered his skin. She felt him draw in his breath at her touch before he gently pulled her hand away.

"My boots," he said. He sat down hastily, tugging at his footwear. That mission accomplished, he stood up, pulling his shirt over his head and flinging it across the room.

"Now," he said, with an enticing smile. "Where were we?"

Emily reached out again to trace her fingers across his chest, her hand trailing down to cross his tautly muscled abdomen. "If I am beautiful, you are too," she said.

Hart laughed, a low rumble that rippled through his chest. "Flattery will gain you something, my dear Emily," he said, as he lifted her up and set her upon the bed.

In a moment her chemise and his breeches were gone, and he stretched out next to her, his body hard and lean and warm against hers. Emily could not get enough of the feel of him—a man's body—beneath her fingers. He was so solid, so . . . comforting. But her coherency of thought drifted away beneath the onslaught on her senses.

She had known what she wanted when she invited him into her bed—the security of a man beside her, the comfort of his arms wrapped around her. Emily had not thought beyond that to the exquisite sensations he was producing in her—sensations only dimly remembered after years of celibacy. But Hart skillfully brought those long-dormant passions back to life, with such strength that she wondered briefly if it had even been this powerful with Stephen.

Hart's hands and mouth seemed everywhere, inflaming her almost to the point of madness. Her breasts were heavy, her nipples hard, under his ministrations. She wanted to cry out to him to stop, that she could not endure it any longer, but a new wave of pleasure washed over her and drove any thought of escape from her mind.

Emily started with shock and desire when he gently touched her at the apex of pleasure, then melted into his hand as he stroked her into further flame. She clutched at his shoulders while he nuzzled at her breasts, her body responding with a forcefulness that stunned her. Her pleasure climaxed and she cried out her joy.

"Yes, yes, Emily, let me hear your pleasure," he whispered against her ear as his hand continued to send her aquiver.

"Hart," she managed to gasp before his mouth came down on hers, his tongue probing and seeking in imitation of the delight that she knew was coming. She clung to him, fully returning his ardor, wondering that she could even respond after he had brought her to such heights. But skillfully, passionately, he stoked the fires anew until she was ready to beg him to complete their union.

He drew back then, looking down into her face. In the dim light, his eyes glittered like blue fire. "I want you, Emily," he said, his breathing harsh and ragged. "I want to be inside you, filling you, feeling you."

"Oh, yes, Hart, yes!" she gasped.

He nudged her legs apart, positioning himself between them. Clasping her buttocks, he eased himself into her softness.

"So tight," he murmured. "Dear God, Emily, you feel so good." His lips moved over her neck as he slowly moved within her.

Emily marveled at how they moved together as if they had been lovers for a lifetime. The thought fled as quickly as it came, replaced with a growing anticipation coursing through her veins. She tossed her head back and forth in growing rapture.

"Oh, yes, Emily, surrender to it." Hart's voice was harsh with desire.

She gave herself up to him, enfolded him, held herself to him as his thrusts grew uneven, his breathing labored. Then that familiar swell of sensation coursed through her and she heard herself moaning his name again and again. His thrusts quickened, then suddenly a waft of cool air swept over her as he pulled back. The warm, sticky wetness against her thigh told of his self-control.

"Thank you," she whispered, chagrined that she had not thought through all the possible consequences of her actions.

Hart propped himself up on one elbow and brushed the damp tendrils of hair from her brow. "Somehow, I do not think a pregnancy would greatly enhance the reputation of Lincolnshire's Lady Darrow," he said with a wry smile.

Emily laughed and reached out to stroke his cheek. "Ever concerned for my reputation," she teased. "You make a sadly conventional rake, Hart."

He planted a soft kiss on her brow and gathered her into his arms.

13

Emily awoke with a start, instantly aware that she was alone in the bed. She glanced about the room but the duke was gone. Of his clothes, which had been strewn about the room in careless abandon last evening, there was no evidence. Her own clothing was neatly draped over a chair, where it certainly had not lain last night. Had Hart done that?

She lay back against the pillows, welcoming the aching soreness of her muscles. They had indulged their passion once again during the night—slowly, with greater care and even more satisfaction. Emily entertained no regrets; she had needed him last night. Wanted him. As he had wanted her.

Despite his aggravating nature and arrogant ways, Emily was drawn to him. Perhaps it was all tied up with this crazy journey, but Hart brought out a sense of freedom in her that she found invigorating and arousing. Emily had felt the smoldering sexual attraction between them for days. At first she ascribed it to his reputation—the Duke of Hartford was known far and wide as a man fond of women in every shape and form. His flattering banter had shown him to be a master of the art. But as their journey progressed, she recognized the spark for what it was—her own deep attraction to him. The thought brought a faint smile to her face. She had certainly put her brother-in-law in his place when he had proposed an 'arrangement of conve-

nience' with her. Yet she had not hesitated to take Hart
into her bed.

She was only with him for this brief moment in time.
Until the boys were found, returned to school, and they
went their separate ways. It was merely something that
she needed—wanted—deserved—a memory she could
draw on during the long, lonely nights that stretched out
before her. She was entitled to a few moments of pleasure to lighten her days. And Lord knows, she thought,
Hart was a most willing accomplice. He would be able
to see this for what it was—a brief interlude—and
would easily let her slip from his life again. With her
living retired in Lincolnshire, there would be no awkward meetings at the homes of friends or at the theater.
She would probably never see him again after this.

And that was precisely the reason she had surprised
even herself with her bold offer. She was safe with
him, for she knew he wanted nothing more than a ca-
sual dalliance. That was his way with all women. And
she did not wish anything more from him. She had no
desire to submit to his control. This had been a moment of wild recklessness, but she wanted it to be
without complications, or guilt, or vague dreams of a
future. For they had no future. Only a few fleeting moments of present.

Tossing back the covers, Emily gingerly stepped
from the bed and reached for her chemise. Upon the table, next to her traveling case, lay a folded piece of paper. Curious, she unfolded the message.

My Emily,
You were sleeping so peacefully I did not wish to wake
you. I have gone to the docks to look again for the
miscreants. Our landlady has offered the services of
one of the maids to accompany you to town if you so
wish.

Affectionately,
Hart

Emily smiled tenderly. Hart could be thoughtful when he wished. It had never occurred to her to explore Bristol. But she would go mad if she stayed at the inn all day, waiting for news of the boys. He had been adamant about her staying away from the docks, but she could at least walk to the high street, and perhaps visit the cathedral. It was a much better alternative than sitting here thinking about Jeremy—and Hart.

Hart paced up and down the docks. The packet boat only made the crossing to Ireland twice a week, and the ticket agent assured him that the boys had not left on the last boat. The next sailing was on the morrow, but there were so many other ships and fishing vessels and God knew what else in the harbor that those scamps could have talked their way onto.

He had to believe what he'd told Emily—that the boys had not yet reached Bristol. The alternative was too awful to contemplate. For a moment, he wondered if he should have followed their path down the canal more closely. Who knew what might have struck their fancy on the journey? They might have abandoned their plans to visit Ireland entirely.

Then he smiled to himself. If they were so determined to reach their destination that they had passed up the chance to join the traveling fair, nothing was going to deter them from their objective. They would be here eventually. All he had to do was be ready when they arrived.

He met one of the Runners in a less-than-savory wharfside tavern for lunch. The news was good, in a way—the two young boys had not been seen anywhere. Still, the first sense of disquiet crept up on his heart. Perhaps it would be best to track down that canal boatman and find out just where the boys had left him. He sent the Runner back to Wiltshire with that express goal.

After the Runner departed, Hart sank back in his

chair, nursing his ale. The ticket office for the packet was still closed for the midday break; there was no need to hurry back. It would give him a chance to think about Emily.

Emily. He could not have been more amazed at her actions if she had danced naked through the streets of Bristol. Yet his surprise at her sudden offer had been instantly replaced with a rush of desire that almost overwhelmed him. Despite his recognition of his attraction to her at Tring, he had never thought matters would go this far. During the hours of pleasure last night, he began to see why his old friend Darrow had been so content to abandon his bachelor excesses after marriage. The duke felt a twinge of envy at the thought.

He knew Emily to be a strong-willed, independent woman. To his delight, those tendencies carried over into bed, where she was both softly yielding and highly demanding. Lord, if he had had such a wife as that— full of passion, of fire . . .

She had been touchingly vulnerable as well last night. And he knew he had taken advantage of it. He could have held her and talked and soothed her fears without falling into her bed. But he did not think she had any regrets over what happened. He had been careful to make certain there would be no complications for her in the future. She would be able to return to Lincolnshire without shame or embarrassment.

But was he so certain that he wanted her to return to her home? Hart acknowledged that once the boys were found and returned to school, it would mean the end of this journey across England, spent in out-of-the-way inns, eating modest food, and arguing over the best route to follow. He realized with a sudden pang that he would miss all that.

No, he thought with a new certainty, he would not miss the uncomfortable journey. It was Emily he would miss. And Hart knew he could no more go back to London without her than he could without Phillip.

The more he thought about it, the more determined he grew. It was foolish for her to return to the rundown estate in the north. She had no business bothering herself with such a chore—they could hire a manager to oversee the property until Jeremy came of age. Emily had better things to do than worry about crops and tillage practices and corn prices.

A whole new plan unrolled in his mind. Emily should have someone to take care of her, to keep her from need and want. Someone to dress her in fine clothes and jewels, and allow her to perform no task more strenuous than planning the menu for an elegant society dinner.

It would take some getting used to, of course, after his years alone, but he would not mind. Nothing could be worse than the hell with his first wife. Just knowing he would have Emily in his bed would override any manner of minor inconveniences. And with her financial worries taken care of, there would be no reason for her to maintain her independent ways. She would learn to rely on him and become a most amiable companion. Most amiable. His body tensed at the thought.

He grinned. He was acting as randy as an Oxford undergrad out on his first spree. It took all his willpower to keep himself from dashing out the door, racing back to the inn, and dragging his passionate Emily into bed once again.

Tonight, he promised himself. Treats postponed were sweeter treats. And in this burst of enthusiasm, he must not forget the whole reason for their being in Bristol—Phillip and Jeremy. There was no chance they would slip through his net now, but he wanted to be there when they arrived all the same. The privilege of confronting them face-to-face was something he felt they owed him and he was not going to let anything or anyone keep that from him.

And Emily would look ever so lovely later this evening, with their darkened chamber lit only with the faint glow of candles. Her silken skin would be soft and smooth beneath his fingers . . .

He groaned audibly. Yes, he could wait. For a while.

"I'm hungry," Jeremy said. "Let's eat."

"Where?" Phillip asked. "I haven't seen a likely place anywhere."

"There's bound to be something nearer the center of town," Jeremy told him. "It can't take us long to find. Bath is not that large."

"I still think we ought to travel by the river to Bristol," Phillip said.

"I am sick of traveling on stupid slow boats," Jeremy said. "As soon as we eat, we need to take to the Bristol road and find ourselves a ride."

Phillip scowled, but followed Jeremy down Bath's narrow, hilly streets.

They found a pie vendor in the market and bought their lunch, taking it to the bank alongside the Pultney Bridge to eat.

"Look at those!" Phillip exclaimed, admiring the ducks swimming into view. "Let's give them some of our bread. It's getting hard and stale anyway."

Jeremy was reluctant to give away anything they might need, but he had to admit they needed some fresh bread before they continued on to Bristol. It might involve a mad rush to find the boat once they arrived, and he knew they did not dare board the packet without an ample supply of food. They would replenish their provisions in Bath.

Phillip scrambled down the bank, vainly trying to toss crumbs into the middle of the channel. Jeremy came up behind him and tossed a sizable chunk of bread toward the lead duck, who paddled over to inspect it. The others followed and they finally came within range of Phillip's throwing arm.

The boys enjoyed feeding the ducks for some minutes, but when the bread ran out, the ducks swam away, quacking their annoyance, and the two boys clambered up the bank again.

"Let's go back to the market and get some food for the trip, and then try to find a ride to Bristol," Jeremy said.

Phillip looked about him with consternation. "My bag! It's gone!"

"What do you mean, it's gone?"

"It's gone, stupid. It was lying right here and now it is not."

Jeremy, whose own bag had been tied about his waist, looked down to the bare patch of ground Phillip indicated. "It probably rolled down the embankment," he said. "Let's look around for it."

They searched with ever-increasing urgency for some minutes, but there was no evidence of Phillip's bag to be found.

"What are we going to do?" he wailed. "We will not be able to continue our journey!"

"Shut up, or you will have everyone looking at us," Jeremy said coldly. He could not believe Phillip had been so careless as to lose all his money. The thought that they would have to give up their quest when they were so close to the end caused a strange lump to form in his throat.

He sat down on the grass again and untied his own bag. "Let's see how much money we do have," he said. "Did you tuck some away in your pockets or your shoes?"

Phillip turned out both his pockets, where they found a few sixpence and a shilling. Jeremy drew out his carefully horded cache.

"How much money do we need to get to Ireland?" Phillip asked, fighting back the tears.

"I don't know," said Jeremy. He counted his money

again, even though he knew how much was there. "But I don't think we will have enough for the boat."

"We've got to," Phillip said. "I'm not going to turn back now. Why, we are almost in Ireland."

"You might have to swim if you are going to get there," Jeremy said.

"We can find some way to get more money," Phillip said, brightening. "Someone will be glad to hire two willing boys to run errands or perform some minor tasks."

"I doubt that."

"Well, what do you want to do? Just give up and go back? Some adventurer you are."

"We may as well go on to Bristol," Jeremy said slowly. "No point in giving up until we know for certain."

"That's the spirit," said Phillip, jumping to his feet. "Let's go. The sooner we get to Bristol, the sooner we can go about finding someone who wants to hire our services."

Jeremy did not think they would be so fortunate, but he followed his friend toward the Bristol road. Maybe some sort of miracle would occur before they reached the boat and they would have enough money for passage after all. He could not abide the thought of failing after they had come so far.

The duke did not return to the inn until dinnertime, hoping against hope that the boys would turn up at the last minute. But when the ticket agent finally escorted the duke out the door and locked it, saying he would see him on the morrow, there was nothing else to do but return to the inn.

And Emily. His steps quickened as he hastened up the Broad quay. It was not exertion but anticipation that caused his pulse to race.

She was sitting in the parlor that connected their two rooms, busily sewing. Hart paused quietly in the doorway and watched her with appreciative eyes. She had not pinned up her hair and it lay about her shoulders in lustrous, curling waves. There was a softer look about her face today; the lines of worry and concern had been wiped away.

"You look far too intent on your work, Emily," he said, tossing his coat over the chair.

Emily jumped up eagerly, stuffing a half-embroidered handkerchief into her bag. "Did you learn anything?"

"They are not here yet," he said. "But," he continued more cheerfully, "if they are traveling at the pace we reckoned, they will not arrive here until tomorrow."

Emily smiled bravely. "I know. Still, I had hoped . . ."

Hart stepped closer and took her hand. "It cannot be much longer now," he said.

She nodded.

"Have you eaten? I stayed at the packet office until they closed, but I did not wish you to go hungry in my absence."

"I had a delicious lunch," Emily said.

Hart rang for the landlady and ordered their dinner. "Did you get out to see any of Bristol?" he asked as he loosened his cravat.

"I did," said Emily. "The cathedral was very grand and had some particularly beautiful windows."

"I am glad you found something to occupy your time. Two of the Runners will stay at the packet office during the night, so we will know if those rascals arrive."

Hart poured Emily a small glass of claret and filled a larger one for himself. He paused before he handed it to her. "Did you miss me today?" he asked.

His eager little-boy expression brought a smile to Emily's face and erased what latent nervousness she had in his presence.

"I think it should be I who asks such a thing," she

said. "Certainly, a duke of your stature knows that the absence of his presence is always a deprivation for any lady."

The duke laughed and hugged her close. "You are a treasure, Emily," he said, dropping a soft kiss on her brow. He brushed back a falling lock of her hair, then trailed his lips down her cheek until they reached her mouth. "A treasure," he murmured. Then he was kissing her with all the pent-up passion he had fought against during the day.

It was fortunate, Emily thought, that the landlord knocked on the door to announce dinner, or they might never have eaten their evening meal. She took a sip of wine to restore her composure while the food was laid out upon the table.

Sitting across the table from Hart did nothing to still Emily's fluttering pulse, for the smoldering looks he flashed her while they ate only inflamed her senses. She found her anticipation growing with each bite she took. They had so little time left together and she wanted to take advantage of every moment. Without regrets. Or regard for anything but her own needs.

Hart lay back against the pillows, Emily encircled protectively in his arms. He caressed her naked back.

He did not wish to talk to her yet of his plans. He knew that Jeremy must be returned to her first before she could even begin to think about the future. He grinned wryly. One more thing he could hold against their sons. But he sensed that the chase was nearly over, and he could soon embark on this new course in his life.

Amazing how much change had come into his life in such a short time. Since the day Louisa died, he had sworn he would never remarry, unless, God forbid, it was necessary to ensure the succession. And when he had left London on the way to Norfolk, he had never thought he would find a woman who could so change his mind. But he had, and was glad of it. Emily was the very thing he needed in his life—a lady to cosset and protect, one who would preside over his table, manage his house, and make his nights glorious.

Lord, there would be a million things to do when he returned to London. He would have to settle with Michellene, of course. She could keep the little house in Chelsea—he could afford to be generous, and she had been the most satisfactory of mistresses. There would be solicitors to talk with and settlements to draw up. He would no doubt need to speak with Emily's father—old Burford, wasn't he?

Should he go to her father, hat in hand, asking permission to court his daughter? The thought caused him to laugh aloud.

"What do you find so amusing?" Emily asked sleepily.

Hart planted a kiss atop her head. "Hush," he said, hugging her tight.

He could not imagine a father in the country who would not trip all over himself in his hurry to wed a daughter to the Duke of Hartford. Perhaps he could settle the matter simply by letter. After all, he would marry Emily whatever her father's thoughts on the matter. There was no need to worry about her family until the wedding.

The wedding. It would be a small affair, of course. With as much as there was to do, there was no need for the hasty device of a special license. He was making very certain that Emily would not be blessed with an untimely pregnancy. Perhaps a small ceremony in the chapel at Stratton would suffice. Yes, that would do very well indeed. A minimum of fuss, with only the immediate family in attendance.

Then he would whisk her away on a wedding trip that she would never forget. They had the entire Continent to explore. They need not return for months; winter in Italy could be very pleasant. With the boys safely tucked away at school, there would be no need to worry about them. Emily deserved to have a wedding trip befitting her new rank of duchess.

Duchess. He liked the sound of that. Emily, Duchess of Hartford. Her grace, the Duchess of Hartford. Emily. Dear, sweet, passionate Emily. Just the scent of her intoxicated him and he felt his groin tightening again at the mere thought of having her in his bed every night. And morning. And every minute in between if he so desired.

The more he thought on it, the more he liked the idea of having a wife again. It was so much more convenient than having a mistress. One could not keep one's mistress in the house, so there was always the bother of having to go out. Now, he need not leave the house ever. Emily would be there with him all the time. And on those nights when he was lured away to his club, or to a gathering at the home of one of his cronies, he would know that Emily would be waiting for him when he returned home.

That thought put a smile on his face. He glanced fondly at the woman in his arms, listening to the soft breathing that marked her sleep. He was well pleased with himself. Who would have thought that Phillip's rash escapade could have led to such a satisfying conclusion?

14

Hart was fully awake by the time the second knock sounded on the outer chamber door. Carefully easing his way out of bed so as not to wake the sleeping Emily, he shrugged on his shirt and breeches and slipped into the sitting room. Pulling the hall door open, he beheld one of the Runners.

"Two young lads showed up an hour or so ago at the packet-boat office. The night watchman let them in. We've got a man watching to make sure they don't leave."

Hart's face broke into a broad smile. "Good work."

He finished dressing with hasty carelessness and led the Runner down the stairs. "I wish you to stay here," the duke said. "As soon as the lady awakens, let her know that the boys are found and I shall be returning with them shortly." The man nodded.

Not wanting to waste an instant, Hart did not wait for the horses to be put to the carriage but set out for the docks on foot. It was faster this way. The sky glowed with a pre-dawn light that made this less-than-salubrious area of Bristol look dreamy and peaceful. Hart barely noticed as he raced toward the boat office, his steps quickening as he neared the docks.

It was hard to believe that the chase was over, that the boys were found at last. Hart could not wait to see the ecstatic look on Emily's face when he brought Jeremy to her.

The watchman was waiting for Hart when he reached the yard.

"I hope these are the young lads you be looking for," the man said as he unlocked the outer door.

"So do I," said the duke, striving to keep his emotions under tight control. There was no guarantee it was Phillip and Jeremy who waited inside. If it was not . . .

"They're in there," the watchman said, nodding at the cold, stark waiting room with its hard wooden benches. Hart pressed a generous amount of coin into the man's hand without even knowing how much it was.

Pushing open the door, Hart stood on the threshold, peering into the dimly lit room. Two small bodies were slumped against each other on one bench. In the faint light from the windows he could just make out the blond hair of one and the dark hair of the other. With a deep sigh, Hart let out the breath he had not realized he was holding. He had found them at last.

He stepped into the room, and the dark-haired figure on the bench stirred and looked up. He glanced at the duke with sleepy eyes, which grew wider as they focused on him.

There was no question who the lad was. It was like looking into a reflection of Emily's face. The same dark, curling hair, the same hazel-tinted eyes. There was perhaps a hint of Stephen in the chin and mouth, but Jeremy was unquestionably Emily's son.

"Viscount Darrow?" the duke inquired, with a mocking arch of his brow. "I believe we have not been properly introduced. I am the Duke of Hartford."

Jeremy looked at him, first with surprise, then apprehension. After a moment, he reached over and shook his companion. "Phillip," he said in a loud whisper.

Phillip grunted an acknowledgment, but did not stir.

"I think you had better wake up," Jeremy said, shaking him again.

"Why?"

"Because there is someone here who wishes to speak with you," the duke said sternly.

At the sound of his father's voice, Phillip sat bolt upright, staring at the duke with a mixture of relief and alarm on his face. Since the duke continued to frown, both boys scrambled to their feet.

Hartford turned toward Jeremy. "Do you have any idea of the pain you have put your mother through for this last fortnight?" he demanded harshly. "You are a titled peer, yet you have been off gallivanting around the countryside, making your poor mother sick with worry—"

"Is Mama ill?" Jeremy asked, his eyes wide with concern.

"No, but it is a miracle she is not, as worried as she has been about you," the duke replied. He turned to Phillip, who straightened up under the duke's censorious gaze. "As for you, young man ... What do you have to say for yourself?"

"I am sorry, sir," Phillip said, his eyes locked on his toes.

"You are sorry?" the duke said, his voice heavy with sarcasm. "You left school without permission, put yourself in untold danger cavorting around the countryside in the company of all manner of rogues, were preparing to leave the country, and all you can say is 'I'm sorry' ?"

"It is my fault, too," Jeremy interjected.

The duke quelled his tongue with a searing look. "Never in all my life have I heard of two boys misbehaving as badly as you two. Your father and I were known for our pranks in our younger days, but we never—never—did anything that would bring such worry to our families."

"There was no need to worry," Phillip said cheerfully. "We were fine."

"Someday," said the duke with a warning glance,

"when you have children of your own, I can only hope you will finally gain some appreciation of the severity of your crime."

Phillip looked back to his toes again.

Hart gestured at the lumpy bag on the bench. "Is that yours?"

Phillip and Jeremy nodded.

"Take it up and come with me, then," the duke said. "No doubt you would like your breakfast. I look forward to the opportunity of eating mine with a peaceful mind at last."

"Can you help me send a letter to Mama?" Jeremy asked as he picked up his bag. "I did not think she would be so worried, and I'd better let her know I am safe."

"You will shortly have the opportunity to personally inform her of your safety," the duke said, motioning them toward the door.

Phillip and Jeremy shared a surprised look. Jeremy picked up his bag, and they followed the duke out of the room. They struggled to keep up with his long, loping stride as he led them back to the inn.

"I think he's real mad," Jeremy said in a subdued tone.

"I hope not," Phillip replied. "Else I'm going to get it. You're going to get it too, if your mother is here."

"I'm glad she is here."

"We almost did it, you know," Phillip said sadly. "If Papa had not found us . . ."

"We didn't have enough money for the passage," Jeremy pointed out. "Didn't you see the sign on the wall? It's a good thing your papa did show up."

"I'm still going to go to Ireland someday," Phillip vowed.

Jeremy smiled. "We'll go together. After we leave Oxford."

"Cambridge."

"Oxford."

The boys were once again in high spirits when they reached the inn. Hart herded them up the stairs and pushed them into the sitting room that he shared with Emily. Briefly, he wondered if he should have left them downstairs while he broke the news to Emily. There was no telling how she would react.

"Hart?"

He glanced up and saw her standing in the doorway to her room, an expression of disbelief on her face. Hart nudged Jeremy forward.

Emily clapped a hand over her mouth to stifle her gasp of surprise and delight. "Jeremy!" she cried, racing toward her son. She threw her arms around him in an exuberant hug. "Oh, Jeremy, it is really you!"

"Hello, Mama," he said, his pleasure at seeing his mother warring with his male reluctance to have a fuss made over him. "Why are you here in Bristol?"

"We have been chasing after you two for a fortnight," Hart said. "And I think you should apologize here and now to your mother for all the grief you caused her."

"I am sorry, Mama," Jeremy said. "I did not want you to worry. I tried to write you a letter, but the lockmaster wouldn't give me any paper, and then we lost all of Phillip's money in Bath and . . ." His expression turned rueful. "I should not have left school, really."

"No, you shouldn't have," the duke said.

Jeremy began to look embarrassed by all her attention, so Emily reluctantly released him, but could not resist the impulse to run her hand through his tangled brown curls. She examined him critically, noting his dirty and worn clothing, at which she shook her head. Still, he was the most welcome sight she had ever beheld.

"A little worse for wear, but no permanent damage, I think," said Hart. He stood behind Phillip, his hand resting lightly on his son's shoulder.

Emily looked up at Hart. "Thank you," she whispered, the tears glistening in her eyes. "Oh, Hart, thank you." She took a step toward him, wanting to hug him with the same intensity she had Jeremy, but drew up short before the watchful eyes of the boys. "I shall never be able to repay you for this."

"It is not necessary," he said, patting Phillip on the shoulder. "We couldn't have found the one without the other." Besides, her radiant smile was all the recompense that he needed at the moment. Later . . . well, he could think of a more pleasurable method of thanking him. "I think the first order of the day is breakfast," he said, looking at the two boys. "Then we need to procure a bath and some decent clothes for these fellows." He glanced at Emily, as if seeking confirmation for his words. She nodded.

Emily could not tear her eyes away from Jeremy while the four ate breakfast, as if afraid he would disappear again if she did not always keep him in sight. He looked thinner, and tired. But there was also a newfound look of maturity about him.

The boys busied themselves with stuffing their faces with as much food as they could. Emily wondered how long it had been since they had eaten a decent meal. Yet even in their hunger, they were eager to talk about their adventure.

"We saw the most amazing things, Mama," Jeremy said between mouthfuls. "There was a fair in one place and we even got to hold the snake! They fed him a rabbit that looked just like Peter at home."

"Can I get a pet snake?" Phillip asked the duke. "We could feed him rabbits from the woods."

"No."

"We rode on a canal boat," Jeremy told his mother. "It was fun for a while, but they go so slowly! We got to see the big white horse carved into the hill. The boatman said it's been there for ever so long—maybe even before Roman times."

"Like your stupid road," Phillip said. "I still can't

believe that Roman soldiers would have marched down that boring thing."

"Well, it was probably more fun with a whole army," Jeremy retorted.

"Did you pass through Oxford?" the duke asked, remembering the rumor they had heard.

Phillip nodded. "That was my idea. But it was boring. Do I have to go to college when I get older? I did not think either Oxford or Cambridge looked like much fun."

"Yes, you will have to go and you will not be there to have fun," the duke said with a stern look. "You will be there to obtain an education and learn the qualities of a gentleman." He frowned as Phillip grabbed for another piece of bread. "Something I feel you are sorely lacking at this moment. Have you forgotten all your manners?"

Phillip looked shamefaced and put down the bread.

"However did you find us?" Jeremy asked as he forked another slice of ham onto his plate.

"You can thank providence," said the duke. "And Robert Mayfield."

"What did Robbie do?" asked Phillip. "He didn't know anything about our plan."

"It seems that Mr. Mayfield overheard an argument between you two which indicated that Ireland might be your planned destination."

"We almost got there," Phillip said with pride.

"What is this you said about losing your money in Bath?" Emily asked.

Phillip flushed. "It was my fault. And my money. Jeremy took good care of his."

"How were you going to buy passage to Ireland if you had no money?" Emily asked.

"We thought we might have enough," Phillip explained. "Or if we did not, we figured we could earn more running errands around the docks or something like."

Emily shuddered at the thought. They were so young and inexperienced to be out in the world. It was a miracle no harm had befallen them.

She glanced over at Hart, who was eating with his usual enthusiastic appetite. He did not seem at all like a man who had just found his missing son, but she noted the relieved looks he kept giving Phillip and realized he was not so blasé about the reunion as he pretended. There was a father's love reflected in his eyes.

Following breakfast, steaming kettles of water were brought to Hart's bedroom. The duke ordered the boys to scrub themselves until they were so clean they squeaked. Emily retreated to her own chamber, coming out only to accept the bundle of clean clothing the landlady brought. An hour later, freshly washed and dressed, the boys sat before her. Hart had gone out to make preparations for the return journey.

Emily looked at Jeremy. "Whyever did you decide to do such a thing?" she asked.

Jeremy flushed guiltily. "Phillip called me a liar," he said, "and I had to prove to him that he was wrong."

"Was running away the best way to settle the matter?" she asked.

"No." Jeremy hung his head. "Are you going to punish me?"

"A man is always ready to accept the consequences of his actions," Hart interjected as he came into the room.

"You won't ... you won't take me out of school, will you?" Jeremy asked in a pleading voice. "I promise never to run away again."

"That decision may be up to your uncle," Emily said, although she fully intended that the man should never hear of this escapade. "He may not want to have his money wasted in such a manner."

"You are not going to take me out of school, are you, sir?" Phillip asked, darting an apprehensive look at his sire.

"Do you think it would be a just punishment for your irresponsible behavior?" the duke asked.

"No, sir," Phillip replied honestly.

"I shall think on the matter," said the duke. He turned to Emily. "I have engaged a post-chaise and we will be able to leave shortly after luncheon," he said. "I can promise you a more comfortable journey this time."

"Are you coming with us?" Phillip asked.

"Yes," the duke said. "I do not wish to burden Lady Darrow with the responsibility of ensuring your good behavior. You will not be out of my sight again until you have reearned my trust and respect."

"Yes, sir," Phillip mumbled. He and Jeremy retreated silently to the two wooden chairs flanking the window.

"Do not move from that spot," the duke commanded. Taking Emily's elbow, he led her into the first bedroom.

"I assume you wish Jeremy to go back to school," he said in a decisive manner. "It should not take us more than three days to reach Norfolk."

"Do you intend to return Phillip to school?"

The duke gave her a puzzled look. "Of course. What else would I do with him? Let Elston keep his high spirits corralled."

"I thought that perhaps after this you would keep him at home, with a tutor."

The duke frowned. "I think he is best off in school. I do not think Elston can be faulted for the boys' folly."

Emily nodded her agreement. "I certainly want Jeremy back there." She walked to the window and glanced down at the street below. "I can hardly believe that we have found them at last. It seems as though we have been chasing those two across England forever. Yet it was only ten days."

"I am certain you look forward to returning to a more normal existence," he said. "I know I do."

Emily turned and looked at Hart. "I cannot ever thank you enough, Hart. For finding them. And allowing me to accompany you. I know . . . I know I was not always an amiable companion."

Hart stepped toward her and took her hand. "You were more than amiable, Emily." His eyes lit with an appreciative gleam. "Delightful, in fact. Most delightful."

Emily knew he would kiss her next and she deftly stepped aside. At that moment she realized that with the boys' arrival something precious had vanished in their wake—her easy relationship with Hart. He was once again the Duke of Hartford, and she was the impoverished Lady Darrow. Their magical time was over. She smiled sadly as Hart went out into the sitting room.

She had known, of course, that things could not go on as they had been once the boys were found. But she had not expected them to change so instantaneously either. Emily was surprised to find that she felt a lingering sadness for something that she had always known could not last.

Suddenly, the thought of spending any more time with Hart seemed intolerable. If she had enough money of her own, she would immediately have rented a separate carriage for herself and Jeremy. But she already owed the duke more money than she dared contemplate; a carriage was a luxury she could not even dream about.

So she would put on a smiling face, allow the relief she felt at finding her son to seep into her being, and find some way to endure the trip homeward. She had Jeremy back, and nothing could dim the relief she felt at that. But she knew the return trip to Norfolk would be nothing like the journey to Bristol. The enchantment was gone.

Her trip with Hart had been a magical adventure and she was sorry to see it end. If only she could have had a few more days with him ... But the boys were safe and soon to be back in school, and she would be home again. The estate and her garden awaited her. There would be more than enough to do. The sooner she reached home, the better. She had known all along that this was only a temporary respite from life.

Yet why did that small voice inside her insist she wanted it to continue?

Emily had never intended her feelings for Hart to move beyond her immediate need for comfort and security. But the thought of leaving him made her realize how much she truly cared for him.

It was a foolish, silly infatuation on her part. He did not entertain similar feelings for her. She could not expect Hart to fall in love with her simply because she wished him to. They were too vastly different people, from vastly different worlds. There were many things about him that she heartily disliked. He was not at all the type of man she admired and respected.

But she could not keep herself from loving him.

15

They left Bristol in early afternoon in a well-sprung post-chaise, stopping briefly in Bath for a light repast. Phillip reveled in the carriage ride, persisting in hanging out the window and yelling "Spring 'em!" to the coachman at nearly every curve. After the fifth or sixth time, Emily began to think him a rather ill-mannered brat, but Hart only smiled indulgently at his antics. And he thought she was too soft on Jeremy! She was well pleased with the behavior of her son, who sat quietly in his corner of the coach, gazing out the window with well-mannered interest as the countryside sped by.

The carriage rolled on, halting only for a change of horses, then pushing on into the early evening. They did not reach Marlborough until long after the dinner hour.

Emily kept a watchful eye on the boys while Hart arranged for rooms, and a meal. Although the coach was far more comfortable than the open curricle, Hart had ordered the driver to maintain a pace that was no easier than the one they had followed on the way to Bristol. Emily was thoroughly exhausted by the time she sat down to eat.

The boys, who had been subdued during the last hour of the journey, broke into lively, animated conversation at the dinner table. Hartford, growing tired of the din, sent them off to their room the minute they finished eating.

The duke, who felt that in his role as future father he

should make a close examination of Jeremy, thought he had seen much that was good in the lad. But he also told himself that he saw a few examples of Lady Darrow's detrimental feminine influence. Jeremy was not nearly as lively or talkative as Phillip—the obvious result of being raised in a household run by a woman. Still, in time the boy could overcome that handicap.

This would be the perfect opportunity to start exerting his influence.

"There is still a matter I need to take care of with Phillip," the duke said to Emily. "He needs a good thrashing for his misbehavior and I intend to give him one. I will deal with Jeremy for you as well."

"You will deal with Jeremy?" Emily asked indignantly. "At whose behest?"

"You know perfectly well you will not do it and it needs to be done," he said. "This is not a matter for female squeamishness. I think they learned much from their adventure, and thank God they came to no harm in the process. But the boys must learn there is a price to pay for disobedience. It may not keep them from every mischief in the future, but perhaps they will think twice before embarking on anything like this again."

"I am perfectly capable of disciplining my own son," Emily said carefully.

Hart looked at her doubtfully, then shrugged. "As you wish. The landlord informs me he has a goodly supply of switches, for the recalcitrant kitchen boys. I shall send Jeremy down to you."

"Thank you," Emily said icily, infuriated by his interference. She knew he thought her too soft, too yielding. Well, perhaps she was by his standards, but she thought she had done an effective job of raising Jeremy so far. Without his advice or assistance. Phillip certainly demonstrated that Hart's methods worked no better. She had never spanked Jeremy in his life and he seemed none the worse for it.

* * *

Jeremy came into the dining parlor with an apprehensive expression. "Hartford said you wanted to see me," he said.

"Yes, I did," Emily said. "Sit down."

"Are you going to thrash me?" he asked.

"Have I ever thrashed you?"

"No. But Phillip said you probably would. His papa is going to thrash him."

"Do you think it would make you feel any better about what you did if I did thrash you?" Emily asked.

Jeremy shook his head.

"I am greatly disappointed in you," Emily said. "I expected better behavior from my son. First, you were very inconsiderate of Mr. Elston. He is doing his best to run a good school, and having two of his boys run away is certainly not showing any appreciation for the hard work he does. Do you not like the Norfolk Academy?"

"Oh, yes," protested Jeremy. "I like it very much. Elston and the other teachers are good fellows."

"You also demonstrated great disrespect for your uncle. He is providing a goodly sum of money to pay for your schooling, which you are wasting by not being at your lessons."

"I am sorry."

"By encouraging Phillip to go with you, you also caused the duke a great deal of grief and expense. Do you know how many men he had racing about England looking for you? Each and every one of those men had to be paid. Hart also had his own expenses for horses, food, and lodging while he chased you two down."

"Should I repay him?" Jeremy asked.

Emily shook her head. "I would ask it of you, if it were possible. But we both know you do not have access to such a sum. And that brings me to my greatest grievance. I also had to expend a substantial sum of money while looking for you. Money I can ill afford."

"We will not lose the estate, will we?" Jeremy asked anxiously.

"No. But there will be a good many things we shall have to forgo in the coming year because the money is no longer there."

"I will give up my pocket money next term," Jeremy said. "That will help, won't it?"

"Yes, it will. But I cannot have you at such a disadvantage with the other boys. You will have to make the sacrifice elsewhere."

"We can sell my rabbits," Jeremy said reluctantly.

Emily's heart went out to him. He loved his pets and she, being too softhearted, had allowed them to be treated as such instead of serving them at her own table, or selling them to the neighbors. But Jeremy must learn to accept the consequences of his actions.

"I think we need to do that with the next litter," Emily said. "Not Peter, of course. But the next batch of babies can be sold. That will be a start toward keeping you in funds and paying me back."

"Phillip gets five whole pounds every quarter," Jeremy interjected.

"There is no need for a lad of your age to have that much money," Emily said sternly. "You two would never have conceived this wild idea of going to Ireland if you did not have the funds for the journey."

"I am sorry, Mama."

"You can show me how sorry you are by applying yourself diligently when you return to school. You have a great deal of work to make up."

"I'll work especially hard," Jeremy promised. "I will."

"Good." Emily was forced to smile at his earnest expression. "Now, you head up to bed. The duke will be wanting to make an early start in the morning."

"Good night, Mama."

"Good night, Jeremy."

He turned to go, but then ran back and gave her a hug. "I love you."

Emily squeezed him hard. "I love you, too."

She waited a few minutes to allow Jeremy to reach her room; then she herself ascended to her chamber. She did not wish to speak to the duke again this evening.

Those days in Bristol had been an idyllic interlude, interrupted now by real life. All her old apprehensions about the duke rushed back—his domineering and imperious ways, his conviction that she was not doing a good job raising Jeremy, and his male determination to interfere whether he was asked to or not. She wanted to stamp her foot and rail at him for his insensitive attitude.

How had she ever thought him a caring and considerate father? He was still the cold, domineering aristocrat she had labeled him when they first met. In the magic of these past days, she had been temporarily blinded as to his true nature. But now the blinders were off and she saw him as he really was—the type of man who wanted to exert absolute control over everyone and everything around him.

But he could not control her.

Phillip was blinking back the tears in his eyes when Jeremy entered the bedroom. Jeremy cast an apprehensive glance at the duke, who sat on the edge of the bed watching his son.

"Mama said I should go to bed now," Jeremy said.

"A good idea for both of you," said the duke.

Phillip turned to Jeremy. "Did your mama thrash you?" he asked.

Jeremy shook his head. "But I have to sell my rabbits to pay her back the money she spent looking for me."

The duke snorted derisively.

"That doesn't seem half fair," said Phillip. "You didn't ask her to come after you."

"Any young gentleman who takes an unauthorized leave from school can expect his parent to come after him," said the duke. His cool, blue eyes appraised Jeremy in a thoughtful manner. "Now, tell me honestly, Darrow. You know there are no such thing as leprechauns, don't you?"

"Of course there aren't," Phillip shouted gleefully. "I told him they did not exist, but he wouldn't believe me. That's why I wanted to go to Ireland—to prove there weren't any."

The duke silenced him with a quelling stare.

Jeremy glanced about uncomfortably. "I guess . . . I know there aren't."

"Good," said the duke. "Now, we'll have no more nonsense of this sort in the future. Fairy stories are all well and good for children in the nursery, but you are a growing lad who needs to turn his attention toward more important things." His expression grew less stern. "How would you like to visit with Phillip this summer?"

"Could I?" Jeremy asked eagerly.

"I am confident your mother could be persuaded to let you," the duke said with a smile.

"That would be wonderful," Phillip said. "Papa can take us to a mill and to the horse races and—"

"Hold on there. I make no such promises to entertain you. I may have other plans for the summer."

Phillip looked crestfallen. "But Jeremy's never been to anything like that. His mama wouldn't let him. Please say that you will take us."

"I will try, if it is convenient. You two can surely find enough to do around the estate to keep you well occupied."

"You can meet my horse," Phillip told Jeremy. "We can ride out every day."

"I've never ridden a horse," Jeremy said.

"Then it is high time you did," the duke declared. "Your father was a neck-to-nothing rider and I'll wager you can be the same."

"I am not certain Mama will approve," Jeremy said.

"What's she got to do with it?" Phillip asked. "She's not going to be there, anyway."

"Actually, I thought to include Lady Darrow in my invitation," the duke said. Should he take the boys into his confidence yet? No, best to wait until the matter was settled. They would find out soon enough.

"Then we won't be able to have any fun," Phillip said with a glum expression. "You know how mothers are."

"My mama is a right 'un," Jeremy said defensively.

"Yes, she is," said the duke. "And I do not wish to hear you speak disrespectfully of Lady Darrow, Phillip."

"Sorry, sir."

"I will make all the arrangements, then," said the duke as he stood. "You will have a good time, Jeremy."

"Thank you, your grace."

"Please call me Hartford."

"Hartford. Sir."

After the duke had left the room, Phillip turned to Jeremy with glee. "You will be able to visit this summer! We will have ever so much fun!"

"If Mama allows me to come," Jeremy said gloomily. "She is still awfully angry."

"She wouldn't dare say no to Papa," Phillip said with the utmost confidence. "No one says no to a duke, you know."

Jeremy looked doubtful. "Mama just might," he said.

"Then you'll just have to run away again and come to Stratton."

Jeremy shook his head. "No, I do not think I will run

away again. It was fun some of the time, but you know, I am rather glad they found us."

Phillip's face took on a sheepish look. "Me too."

In the morning Emily joined the duke for breakfast. She expected him to inquire about her treatment of Jeremy the previous evening, but he was silent on that subject.

"I had thought to travel only as far as London today," the duke said. "We will be far more comfortable at the house there than at some inn."

"I think it imperative that we get the boys back to school as soon as possible," Emily said, aghast at his suggestion. The thought of spending the night in the duke's London town house horrified her. Now that her adventure was over, she wanted to be back in Lincolnshire as quickly as possible. There was no point in prolonging the inevitable parting.

"We will only lose a few hours' travel," he said. "I doubt that will cause severe harm to their studies. They will be applying themselves to their lessons for the next few weeks to make up for their absence."

"I cannot accompany you to London," said Emily. "Have you forgotten the impropriety of our situation?"

Hart stared at her with fond amusement. "Is this the same Lady Darrow who told me not too long ago that she did not care a fig for her reputation?"

"I did not care for my reputation in small towns like Royston or Tring. London is quite a different matter. If you think you will be able to smuggle us in and out of town without anyone the wiser, you are sadly mistaken. Servants talk, you know."

"Mine do not, if they wish to remain employed. But if you do not wish to make an early stop in town, so be it." Hart did not mind overmuch. He would bring her down to London later, before the wedding. That would be even better, he realized. She needed a new wardrobe, and that would take a great many days to procure. They could take in the late-Season entertainments, then retire to Stratton for the wedding.

Lord, he would have to find a chaperon somewhere if he intended to keep Emily with him the entire time. Which he fully intended to do. Her mother, perhaps? Hart shook his head. He could not quite imagine sharing Emily's bed while her mother was under his roof. He would have to find a less-interested lady to lend them countenance. He certainly had no intention of throwing a sop to propriety by having Emily stay anywhere but under his own roof. She was a widow, after all. As long as there was another female in the house, no one would say a word.

Particularly after he sent the notice to the papers. He almost laughed aloud at the incredulous expressions that would be found about town when the news became known. The gossips would have a field day.

Perhaps he should delay the notice until they had time to deal with Emily's wardrobe. The moment the news was out, the house would be flooded with callers eager to catch a glimpse of the future Duchess of Hartford. He needed to make certain Emily would be decked out in a style befitting her position.

The thought of obtaining a special license and marrying her immediately suddenly grew more appealing. They could be gone to the Continent before anyone was the wiser, and then she could have her choice of the latest Paris fashions.

For a brief moment, he wondered which course Emily would prefer. The latter, no doubt. After all, she had been out of society for a great deal of time. It would not be fair to bring her to town so suddenly, when they would be a nine days' wonder. Better that they made their appearance as duke and duchess after their extended honeymoon trip.

Of course, if things went as he hoped, it might not be possible for Emily to be out in society then. He fully intended to plant a child in her belly before they

returned to England. He rather hoped it would not be
immediately—he knew enough about the travails of
pregnant women not to wish his honeymoon ruined in
that manner. But a temperate winter in Italy would
give him the ideal opportunity to start their new family.

Just the thought of impregnating Emily made his
breathing deepen. It was damn hard being cooped up in
a carriage with her, chaperoned by two inquisitive
young boys. And lying alone in his bed at the inn last
night had not been an easy task, knowing her room
was next to his. He would only have had to slip into
the hall and tap softly at her door . . .

But with the boys present, he dared not indulge his
passion. He was an adult, after all. He could rein in his
desire for a short while longer. Soon he would have
Emily all to himself and he could taste the fruits of her
body whenever he wished. Which would be often, to
make up for his sacrifice now.

Lord, would he ever grow tired of her? He could not
recall a single woman in his past who excited him so.
However could he have thought her plain and insignif-
icant? Emily was a marvel of passion and enticement.
Perhaps because it was so unexpected. She had him
grinning like a giddy schoolboy, struggling to fight
down urges that any normal male could easily contain,
and plotting devious ways to rid himself of two young
chaperons.

The second day of traveling was made at a pace as
hasty as the first. By five that evening, they reached
the outskirts of London. They were met at the Hyde
Park toll gate by the duke's second-best traveling
coach—the one that did not carry the ducal coat of
arms. They transferred from one vehicle to the other,
and traversed the city on the way to the Norwich Road.

Emily could not help but stare out the window as the
coach moved through the busy streets. So much had
changed in the city since she had last visited it. New

bridges crossed the Thames and Regent Street now cut through the heart of the city. For a moment she wished she had accepted the duke's offer to halt overnight in London, but then realized there would not have been time for her to explore in any event.

Someday she would come back. With Jeremy. He needed to experience the delights of London before he grew too much older. Perhaps she could persuade her uncle to invite them for a visit. As much as she hated the thought of putting up with his condemnation of her, she could endure it in order to provide Jeremy with a glimpse of town life. She would never be able to afford to bring him here on her own.

All too soon, the coach reached the edge of the city and reentered the countryside. Emily resisted the impulse to lean out the window to catch one last glimpse of the tall spire of St. Paul's. There was no point in longing after something she could not have.

Instead, she turned her mind to the numerous duties that would be awaiting her when she arrived home. No doubt there would be ample work in the herb garden and stillroom. Workers would have to be hired for the first hay cutting. And she would have to spend long hours going over the books in order to find out exactly where she was going to find the money to repay the duke. Somewhere, it would have to be found. For she intended to reimburse him for every last penny he had expended on her behalf. Emily would not accept charity from her family, and she would certainly not accept it from the Duke of Hartford.

16

They reached the Norfolk Academy late the following day. Elston was all smiles when the duke and Emily deposited their two charges in the headmaster's office.

"See that you do not lose them again," the duke warned him.

"I assure you, we will keep a close watch on them," Elston said. "They shall be too busy with their studies to plot any more mischief."

"I hope so," said the duke. He patted Phillip on the shoulder. "See that you behave yourself. Or I warn you, your summer will be one you shall never forget."

"Yes, sir."

"Take care of yourself," Emily said to Jeremy. "Apply yourself to your studies."

"I will," Jeremy said. "'Bye, Mama."

"Goodbye." Emily fought the urge to give him one more hug; she knew she dare not do so in the presence of the others. She followed the duke out of the room.

"I suggest we return to Norwich for the night," the duke said. "The accommodations will be better there. We can set out for Lincolnshire in the morning."

"You do not need to escort me home," Emily said. "I can certainly get there by myself."

"I will not have you jauntering about on the mail," the duke said insistently. "You will have a proper escort and a proper traveling coach. One that befits a lady."

Emily nodded, knowing it would be pointless to argue with him. How wonderful it would feel to be home at last, where she could do as she pleased without anyone to gainsay her. The duke's protective attitude was beginning to chafe her. It was as if he was once again denying her ability to take care of herself, ignoring the fact that she had managed for eight years on her own.

One more day and she could have her own life again.

When the coach pulled up before one of the grander inns in Norfolk, the duke leaned over toward Emily. "I will bespeak us a bedchamber. Do you wish to have a private sitting room as well?"

Emily stared at him with bemusement for a moment before she realized that the duke intended that things were to go back to the way they had been in Bristol. Dear God. It was too late for that. "I think it would be best if we had separate rooms," she said slowly, frantically searching for a plausible excuse to forestall him. "Norwich is so close to the school . . ."

Hart nodded reluctantly, accepting her decision. He had been here enough times that he could easily be recognized. As they would probably be here many times more over the years, with the boys at Elston's academy, it would not do to stir up gossip now. They would be in the privacy of Emily's home tomorrow. He could wait one more night. After all, there would be no end to their nights after that.

By leaving Norwich shortly after dawn, they were in Lincolnshire by mid-afternoon. Emily found it difficult to dampen her eagerness as the coach neared Longridge. Never since Stephen's death had she been away for so long. She wanted to see its old, familiar walls.

But mixed with her anticipation was a twinge of anxiety and apprehension. She could only guess what Hart would think of the estate and its condition. She

did not want to have a scene with him; she only
wanted him to deposit her at the doorstep and be gone
out of her life again, so she did not have to dwell on
what might have been. Emily prayed that the parting
would be handled amiably between them.

Hart looked about with growing dismay as the carriage slowly bumped its way along the rutted drive.
Raggedy, unkempt hedges marked the edge of the lane,
their branches reaching out to nearly block passage in
some places. He darted a quick glance at Emily, whose
eyes were resolutely fixed on some distant point in
space.

He let out a sigh of relief when the hedges ended
and the lawn came into view. At least, he thought it
had once been the lawn. It looked much more like a
country meadow now. He would not have been surprised to see several cows grazing among the knee-
high grass and flowers that rippled gently in the
breeze.

Looking to the other side, he saw the solid bulk of
the house approaching. He was on his feet the moment
the carriage stopped, flinging open the door and jumping to the ground before anyone could make a move to
help him. He lowered the steps and offered his hand in
assistance to Emily.

As her feet met firm ground again, she lifted up her
eyes to the brick edifice before her and a smile rose to
her lips. "Oh, how good it is to be home!"

Hart looked at the same building, but he could not
duplicate her enthusiasm. It looked solid enough, but
there was no question it had seen better days. The paint
on the windowsills was chipped and peeling. On the
top story, several windows were boarded over altogether. The drive beneath their feet was more grass
than gravel. He had seen empty houses in better repair.

Emily took his arm and led him toward the steps.
"You must not expect a grand welcome," she said in

warning. "We are not accustomed to the arrival of dukes."

He followed her into the dimly lit entry hall, their footsteps echoing on the cold marbled floor. Emily danced up the stairs, while he went up more slowly, making a critical appraisal of his surroundings.

They were intercepted at the top of the stairs by an ancient, stooped man.

"Welcome home, my lady," he greeted.

"It is nice to be home, Harris," she replied. "Jeremy is back at school and none the worse for wear after his adventure."

"I am glad to hear that his lordship is well." The butler cast a curious glance at Hart.

"Did anything of note occur while I was gone?" Emily asked, moving into the drawing room. She set her worn bonnet on a table.

The butler coughed apprehensively. "There was a slight problem with the roof," he began hesitantly.

"Again? Which one this time?"

"'Tis in the ballroom."

Emily let out a relieved sigh. "I can be thankful it was not in a more critical location," she said. "How bad is it?"

"I do not think it will go through the winter without causing extensive damage, my lady."

Frowning, Emily said, "Well, there is nothing we can do about it until fall. I shall examine the problem later. Could you have Mrs. Harris bring tea, please?"

Harris bowed and disappeared.

Hart stood in the center of the room, noting his surroundings with a meticulous eye. The room was nearly bare of furniture—only a modest sofa and two chairs, each flanked by a small table. No pictures hung on the wall; no ornaments decorated the mantel. There was no carpet beneath his feet, either, with the result that every sound was magnified.

He glanced toward the windows, noticing the two

cracked panes and the total absence of any curtains or draperies. My God, how desperate was Emily's situation? "Is the rest of the house like this?" he asked abruptly.

"What do you mean?" Emily asked.

"Bare. Empty. Stripped of anything that has an ounce of value."

She flushed. "I do not often entertain," she said, a defensive look rising in her eyes. "I see no need to waste money on unnecessary decoration."

"How often do you have a problem with the roof?" he demanded.

"We had a bad storm last winter that loosened too many slates," she said matter-of-factly. "I cannot afford to replace the entire roof, so we must patch only those places that leak."

A short, well-rounded woman bustled into the room, carrying the tea tray. "Good day to you, my lady," she said. "It is glad I am to have you back, safe and sound. And Master Jeremy as well."

"I am glad to be back," Emily said.

Hart looked at the teapot, cups, and saucers. Elegant china, but chipped—every one. And instead of the usual tray of tasty treats, there were only some plain biscuits, and a small number at that.

"Tea, your grace?" Emily asked.

"Thank you."

"I am sorry we do not have anything more enticing to eat, but without any notice of my arrival . . . Mrs. Harris is an excellent cook."

"I am certain she is," the duke said. Assuming she had anything to work with.

He perched awkwardly on one end of the sofa, while Emily sat at the other. He took a sip of the tea and nearly spat out the odd-tasting brew.

"What is this?" he demanded.

"Tea," she replied, then covered her mouth in embarrassment. "Oh, I forgot to tell you that I usually drink herbal tea at home. Mrs. Harris naturally assumed ... Here, let me ring and have another pot brought."

"No, no, this is fine," the duke said, eying his cup with a suspicious look. "What type of herb is this?"

"It is a mixture," Emily explained, sipping her own brew with relish. "A bit of chamomile, costmary, and anise."

"An interesting flavor," Hart replied with a dubious look at his cup.

"It is a soothing brew after traveling," she said. "I shall have to show you the herb garden when we are finished. I only hope it has not gone to weeds while I was away."

If it was anything like the rest of the estate, it most certainly would have, Hart thought to himself. Good God, how could Emily exist in a place like this?

He hastily finished his wretched tea and urged her to show him the garden. He resolved to get her out of this house this very evening. They could spend the night at Grantham.

The minute he stepped out the kitchen door, Hart could see the signs of Emily's lavish attention. The front lawn and drive might be a mess, but here all was neat and orderly.

The garden stretched from the kitchen door to as far as he could see. "You manage all of this?" he asked. At Stratton he had an army of gardeners. How could one person manage such a large expanse on her own?

"Mrs. Harris helps with the kitchen garden," Emily explained. "The herbs are mine alone."

As she led him down the bricked walkways, Hart saw that the garden was much bigger even than he had originally guessed. It was divided into neatly planted squares, separated by pathways of brick and gravel. "What is this plant?" he asked, pointing to a purple-headed stem.

"Lavender," she answered, stopping to break off a flower. She pinched the bud and held it under his nose.

"That is the scent," he exclaimed, then looked chagrined. "Your fragrance," he explained. "I like it. Is this the only thing you grow?"

"Oh, no," Emily smiled. "I grow a great variety of things. But I do so love the smell of lavender. I probably grow more than I should."

Looking more closely, Hart noticed that all the plants were not the same. Knowing little of herbs, he did not recognize a one. "You grow everything to sell?" he asked.

She nodded. "For the most part. The apothecary is very pleased with the quality of my herbs," she said proudly.

"But how can you make any money from a few dried plants?" he asked with a bewildered expression.

"They are herbs, not plants. And I simply grow the ones for which the apothecary is willing to pay the most. It is enough to keep the household in funds."

In disarray and disrepair, he thought sourly. "And what of the farms?"

"I lease out the arable land," she said.

"Yet you do not have enough money to fix your roof." He stated the fact baldly.

"There are other things which must come before the roof," she said. "The mortgage, for example. Stephen had drawn heavily against the estate and after he was gone, well, it was our only source of money for some time. But I am managing to pay it off, year by year."

The duke shook his head. She was a fool to try to keep the place going by herself. Better she rented out the house to a tenant who could afford the upkeep. Well, she would not have to worry about that any longer.

"Emily, there is something we need to discuss." He took her hand. "Is there a place were we can sit and be comfortable?"

She nodded and they walked to the far end of the garden. There, low boxwood hedges marked the end of formal cultivation. A stone bench, covered with moss and lichen, sat at the end of the path, facing back toward the house. A massive wall of holly stood behind it, firmly indicating that one was not to go further.

"Originally, there was a large formal garden, very much in the seventeenth-century style," she explained. "Jeremy's grandfather had it uprooted and redesigned. This is all that remains."

"You will like the gardens at Stratton," he said, seating himself beside her.

"Do you ever spend time in your garden?" Emily asked. "It is my favorite place. It is so peaceful, and soothing. Even when I have been working out here all day, I love to sit alone in the evening."

Hart did not think he had ever been alone in any garden in his life. They made for nice strolling on an afternoon or evening, and he had indulged in varied assignations in countless darkened gardens, but he could not recall every going into one just to sit. The thought would never have occurred to him.

"Emily, I cannot bear to think of you living here like this," he began. He gestured toward the house. "Your home is falling down around your ears; you are forced to till the soil like some farm wife. Good God, you are meant for an easier life than this!"

"We are not always free to choose the life we wish," she said stiffly.

"Well, you could certainly choose something better than this. I thought to give you some time in your home, but I see now that it will not do. Come with me now. We can go to Stratton—or London—or Paris, if you like."

Emily closed her eyes against the pain of his words. It was the last thing she had expected. "I fear I cannot accept, your grace."

"It will be an enjoyable time," he said with a cajoling tone. "You need to learn how to enjoy yourself, Emily."

"Several years ago, when I was visiting my sister at Christmastime, I had an interesting conversation with my brother-in-law. He said much the same thing—that it was silly of me to struggle to eke out a living when there were much more pleasant ways to keep myself in greater luxury. I roundly refused his offer."

"Good God, woman, do you think I would take you to my home if I wished to make you my mistress?" Hart demanded with indignation. "We shall marry, of course."

"Oh?"

"Certainly. It is the ideal solution to your problem. You can lease out the estate until Jeremy comes of age. For all you know, he will wish to sell the albatross off when he is older. You need not bother your head about it again. I will take care of everything."

Emily did not respond, so the duke pressed forward. "You yourself said that Phillip could use some feminine influence in his upbringing, and we know Jeremy is without a father. We can join forces and give them both what they need."

Emily struggled to contain her emotions. He was offering what she had never hoped to receive—marriage. But for what reasons? "And what is it that I need?" she asked him.

"A decent home. Freedom from care and worry. Clothes and hats and jewelry in keeping with your station in life, my dear Emily." He took her hand in his. "These hands need never work again."

Emily carefully withdrew her hand from his clasp. "Perhaps there is more to life than luxury and ease."

Hart laughed. "Spoken like one who is trying to reconcile herself to doing without. You need not worry about a thing again, Emily. I will take care of everything."

She fought against the temptation to give in. It

would be so easy to say yes. With Hart, she would be free forever from worry about money and the future—Jeremy's future. Would it be so difficult to allow Hart to take care of them?

But what would be the cost to herself? The loss of her independence, her pride, her identity? Could she give all that up for the security he offered? "I do not wish you to take care of me," Emily said at last. "That is precisely what I do not want. I am my own person, Hart. I do not need you—or anyone—to take care of me."

He gave her the same indulgent smile one would give an adorable but misbehaving child.

"Emily, I wish to take care of you. Women were made to be cosseted and protected. It is one of the things men love to do."

"Not for any selfless purpose, but because it makes you feel superior and noble," Emily retorted. Pity was the one thing she would not accept from him.

"You would prefer life here to what I can offer you?" he demanded, his anger rising.

"It is not *what* you offer, but how you offer it." Emily strove to explain. "Not once have you even thought to ask me what *I* would prefer, Hart. You just jump in, making all these assumptions. As if I did not exist. As if I were a piece of property at your disposal."

"Of course you are not," Hart snapped. He looked at her with impatience. "What precisely is it that you *do* want?"

"I want to be happy," she said. "I want to do what is right for *me*."

"Withering away in Lincolnshire is what is right for you?"

"Compared to other fates I have been offered, it is," she said.

"Living with me would be so miserable?" The hurt showed on his face.

Emily turned away, her fingers twisting around each other in her agitation. "It is not that life with you would be abhorrent, Hart. It is the reasoning behind your offer that I cannot like. You think you are doing me an enormous favor with your generous offer—and perhaps you are. But you cannot see that such an attitude makes your words an insult rather than an attractive option."

"Good God, woman, what do you want? Shall I drop on one knee like some theatrical swain and pledge you my undying love till the end of our days? I certainly thought you were more intelligent than to insist on all that claptrap."

"It is precisely because you are acting like a lovesick swain that gives me pause. You have not thought this through at all."

"What is there to think about? You are poor, I am rich. You are alone, I am alone. Together, we can both be happy."

"You are willing to give up a near-decade of bachelorhood after knowing me for less than a fortnight?" she asked, her expression incredulous. "Pardon me for saying so, Hart, but if that is not impetuousness, I do not know what is."

"Would you have me court you properly? I can certainly do so if that is what you desire." He flashed her a wicked grin. "I merely thought that after all we had shared, we would not wish to waste any more time."

"You mean since you already had me in your bed, you need not expend more effort," she said.

"I said no such thing," he said in a defensive tone. "Although it strikes me as the height of foolishness to act as if you are some green miss making her first bow in society. Good God, Emily, we are already lovers—by your invitation, I may add. You cannot have it both ways."

"You are missing my point entirely. It is not me, Emily, you want, but some female phantasm you have created out of thin air. You think I am she, but I am not."

"Oh?" He arched a supercilious brow.

"No," she said, with a definite toss of her head. "Else you would not natter on about what is best for me, and how beneficial life with you would be."

"All right, coming with me would be the biggest mistake of your life and I shall make you miserable." Hart grinned. "Does that make you feel better?"

"You are the most vexatious man!" she exclaimed.

"That is certainly a case of the pot calling the kettle black," he said. "Stop being unreasonable. Let us go back to the carriage. We have time to find a decent inn in which to spend the night, and tomorrow you can be comfortably ensconced at Stratton."

"Where I will be assigned the role of dutiful wife and doting mother. Excuse me if I am not overwhelmed at the opportunity you offer me."

"My God, you would be one of the premier duchesses in the realm. You certainly have some impractical notions, Emily, but this one is beyond all belief."

"If I am so foolish, why would you even consider marriage to me?" Emily held her breath as she waited for his answer.

"Most of your ridiculous ideas stem from this abnormal life you lead. Once you have been returned to the normal sphere of women, you will be more comfortable and will have no need of these idiotic ideas of yours."

"And what of your idiotic ideas?" she demanded. "Will they disappear also when you become a husband again?"

"What idiotic ideas?"

"Your need to control other people's lives. Your insistence that everyone around you bends to your will. Your total inability to comprehend that not everyone shares your vision of what is right for them."

"You expect me to climb back in my carriage and

leave you here in this . . . this"—he gestured wildly with his arm—"hovel."

"Yes," Emily said with icy control. "That is exactly what I wish you to do."

Hart stared at her as if disbelieving what he heard. His eyes grew cold. "You," he said at last, "are the most foolish woman I have ever met." He turned on his heel and stalked off down the path.

Emily watched him go. She wanted to race after him, to draw him back, to tell him she would go with him anywhere. But a stronger part of her told her she was doing the right thing. They were not meant to be together. Theirs had been a temporary alliance. Nothing would be served by attempting to draw out their affair. It was over; it had never been meant to be a permanent thing. She, in her womanly wisdom, was more far-seeing than he. Someday Hart would realize how foolish his behavior was.

Tears stung at her eyes and she dashed at them with the back of her hand. If only he had said one word about love or affection . . . But he had not. It was far too much of a business arrangement. She would exchange herself for financial security. A very common reason for marrying. But one which was abhorrent to her.

If she did not love him, she might have accepted. But because she did, she could not. For Emily could not imagine anything worse than living with a man who did not return her feelings. There were worse things on earth than living in straitened circumstances. Much worse.

17

The duke seethed with fury all the way to Grantham.
The fact that he was sick and tired of riding in a closed
carriage did nothing to improve his temper. In Emily's
company it had been endurable. Now it was intolerable.

Damn that obstinate woman. He had never met a
more ungrateful creature. Here he was offering her a
life of ease and comfort, and she had the gall to say
she did not want it. Which was laughable. No one
could prefer the life of near-poverty that she lived.

He should return to London and forget about her immediately. But as soon as he thought that, he knew he
could not. He wanted Emily too badly to give up so
soon.

It was merely her pigheaded stubbornness that had
caused her to refuse his plan. Once she had time to
think things over, she would realize what she had denied herself. Soon Emily would be filled with regret
and remorse for what she had done. Hart grinned at the
thought. He wanted her to suffer—only slightly, of
course—for a little while. Just about the time he
guessed she would be filled with despair, he would return to Lincolnshire and take her away for good.

While he waited, he could at least do a few things to
make her life more bearable. The condition of her
house made him shudder. There was no point in spending money on furnishings—they would simply rent it
out unfurnished. But something had to be done about

the roof. It would not take long for serious water damage to result. That would have to be taken care of immediately. He could stay a night in Grantham and arrange things on the morrow. Emily could not say no to an accomplished action.

Would not Emily be surprised?

Emily felt strangely ill at ease for the first few days after her return. She credited it to exhaustion—not until she slept again in her own bed did she realize how tired she was. The first night she slept nearly ten hours. Then there was so much work to be done . . . Mrs. Harris had done a wonderful job tending the gardens, but many plants were ready to be clipped and dried.

Emily only wished she could have found more wearying labor. Clipping lavender stems was not a mentally taxing task, and she found her mind drifting back to the duke far too many times to suit her. Why could she not rid her thoughts of that odious, interfering man?

Ordering her to become his duchess without even a bye-your-leave. No amount of luxury would ever convince her to shackle herself to such a man. She could only imagine the lengths to which he would go to force her into the mold of the woman he wanted her to be. She would lose all her independence, her own opinions, even her rights. As a widow, she was legally her own person. As his wife, she would be his possession.

Emily clipped off the last bit of pennyroyal and straightened. Her gaze drifted toward the house and she froze at the sight. There were men swarming all over the roof. Dropping her basket, she ran toward the house.

"You there! What are you doing?"

One of the men tipped his hat to her, but did not answer. Emily stormed into the house. "Harris? Harris! Where are you? What the devil is going on here?"

"Yes, my lady?"

"Who are those men all over my roof?" she demanded.

"They are here to repair the roof."

"I did not hire anyone to repair the roof. There must be some mistake. Quick, help me get them down before we are forced to pay their wages."

Harris followed her out into the yard. Emily walked to where the men had propped a ladder against the side of the house and began climbing.

"You!" she called when she was high enough to peer over the edge of the roof. "Stop that at once. You are at the wrong house."

"This is Longridge, ain't it?" one workman asked.

"Yes, but I did not hire anyone to repair my roof. Please come down now. I will not pay you for work I did not order."

"We's already been paid for this job, your ladyship. Fix the roof up, nice and tight, we was told. Good thing too, there are some nasty spots up here. Wouldn't stand through another winter a'tall."

Emily shook in frustration. Must she always be plagued with obtuse men? This one was nearly as aggravating as—"Who paid you to fix this roof?" she demanded.

The man shrugged. "We just got sent out on the job."

"Who do you work for?"

"Smithson, out of Grantham."

Emily strove to control her raging temper as she carefully descended the ladder. There was only one person who would have had the audacity to arrange such a thing! The most infuriating, exasperating, arrogant, domineering ...

Emily burst into tears and ran into the house.

Damn him. Damn him! Why could he not leave her alone?

Racing to the sanctuary of her room, Emily slammed the door and sank down onto the bed.

She missed him so very dreadfully. Missed their teasing conversations, his odiously warm insinuations, his messy habits. Her body ached with want for him.

She was no longer the same person who had gone off in such haste to look for her son. Longridge was no longer a refuge for her. She saw the estate with new eyes—Hart's eyes—and it saddened her that she had wasted so much of her life.

She did not begrudge the effort she had expended on Longridge. Jeremy deserved to inherit something. But all the petty sacrifices Emily had made over the years seemed just that—petty. Out of them had come the sin of pride, and with that pride she was now committing the greatest self-sacrifice of all—giving up Hart. For no better reason than her own infatuation with self-denial.

Where had she ever arrived at the notion that she deserved to be unhappy? She did not deserve that at all. She deserved instead the giddy sense of freedom, the happiness, the sheer raw excitement she had felt on that mad journey across England with Hart. He had opened up her eyes to the possibilities before her, and she could not close them again.

But it was not the journey that had brought all that out. It was Hart himself. How could she ever have said no to him? He was impulsive, messy, impatient, and arrogant, but he was also tender, gentle, and caring. Although he tried to dominate her, he could not. She had stood up to him all through the journey and she could stand up to him in marriage as well. Emily had the strength to fight back when he was wrong, and the love to give in when he was right.

With Jeremy, for example. Emily admitted she had guarded him overmuch. Jeremy needed a father who would encourage his boyish inclinations. Emily could trust Hart to do the right thing with her son.

But how was she going to tell him? Had she destroyed her one chance of happiness when she sent

Hart away? And did she have the courage to call him back?

The Duke of Hartford paced up and down his study. He had come down to Stratton in hopes of soothing his frayed nerves, but the peace and quiet of the country-side was even more disturbing than the hustle and bustle of London.

He needed something to do. Boredom nagged at him. Life seemed sadly flat after the excitement of the chase after Phillip. Not that he would ever wish to be on such a mission again, but he had to admit that it had not been boring. On the contrary. "Exhilarating" was the word he would use to describe it.

All because of Emily. Frustratingly independent Emily. He realized with a sudden, desperate need just how much he missed her. And for the first time, he began to have grave doubts that he would be able to per-suade her that she belonged with him.

He had offered her everything he had—money, title, a secure future for both herself and her son, and a beautiful home. Whatever else could she want? She would lack nothing. He would even allow her to rip up a portion of the gardens here at Stratton and grow her blasted herbs if she wished. She could have the final say in all matters dealing with Jeremy, no matter how wrong he thought she was.

Yet he had the nagging feeling that all that would not be enough.

With a clarity that he realized had been lacking in his thinking before now, Hart understood what it was that Emily wanted from him. The one thing he had not offered—the one thing he was not at all certain he could give her. His heart.

He should have seen it from the first. Her marriage with Stephen had been a love match, however sadly it had ended. Her head was still filled with romantical notions that made her think that love was the only foundation for marriage. And that word had never come up between them.

Why could she not be content with what they had? He enjoyed her company and had to admit he even missed her teasing criticisms. They were more than well-matched in bed. Their sons were friends. Emily needed the material things he could provide and he was more than willing to lavish them on her. Why did she have to complicate things by demanding more?

He sat down behind his desk and poured himself a glass of claret. Had he ever really loved any of the women in his life? Louisa, certainly not. He had been fond of her—as fond as one could be of a woman his family had wished him to marry. There were only a few ladies he remembered with special affection.

Like Michellene. So why had he not visited her upon his return to the city?

Because she was not Emily. And right now Emily was the only woman he wished to have in his bed, the only woman whose soft, silky skin he wished to caress, the only woman whose cries of ecstasy he wanted to hear.

The woman he wanted to have in his life forever. The woman he wanted to see with her belly swollen with child—his child, the one he had planted in her during a wild night of loving.

But was that love? He certainly had no inclination to grab a pen and write a sonnet about her beauty or her grace. Not that she lacked either quality, but Hart did not think blathering about them made his admiration greater.

He wondered what she thought about her new roof. Surely it had been installed by now. He met every day in eager anticipation of receiving a scathing denunciation from her for his interference. But nothing arrived in the eagerly awaited post. Was she so angry that she could not even bring herself to write?

She had also not refunded him the monies she owed

him for expenses on the trip. Not that he wanted a penny of it. He'd give the lot to Jeremy, knowing that Emily would not take it back. Did the delay mean that she had reconsidered his offer of help and was willing to let him stand the bill? If so, it was a great step in the right direction. It meant that Emily was willing to accept his help.

And if she could accept his help in that matter, perhaps she could ultimately be persuaded to accept his help in others. He had been overly impatient in his desire to be with her. She only needed more time to adjust to the idea. As much as that frustrated him, he was willing to grant it to her.

Still, when the butler brought the mail in, Hart at once sifted through the letters. A broad grin lit his face when he found the one he was expecting. No question it was from Emily. He broke the seal and scanned the missive.

His smile faded as he read her words. In fact, by the time he was finished, he was scowling.

Damn that woman! He stared at the bank draft he held as if it were some particularly loathsome creature. She had not forgotten about the debt after all. What's more, she included a blistering attack on his unwanted interference in having the roof repaired. She swore she would repay him every penny of the expense. That stupid roofer had been disobliging enough to tell her the amount.

If he were there in Lincolnshire, he would sweep her into his arms and kiss her until she was breathless—and then tell her what a fool he thought she was. How could she continue to be so maddeningly independent?

Yet if she were not, she would not be Emily. And with a start, he realized that it was her independent spirit that he so admired. The fact that she had endured her hardships and deprivations without allowing her spirit to be cowed. Or without sacrificing her delectable femininity. To his great delight, Hart found that

independence in a woman could be maddeningly
arousing. A docile and accommodating Emily would
not be Emily at all.

Was that what love was? Accepting her as she was,
maddening faults and all?

He leaned back in his chair, the grin returning to his
face. They would have a lively time together. It would
not be a peaceful and harmonious existence at all
times. But he thought he would rather enjoy arguing
with Emily on occasion. For after they argued, they
could always kiss and make up. And he thought he
could very easily enjoy that.

Hart glanced at the clock on the desk. Barely past
noon. He could eat a hurried lunch while his valet
packed and be on the road within the hour. He could be
in Lincolnshire tomorrow. And he would have it out
with Emily, once and for all. He would argue, beg, ca-
jole, and plead if he had to. But he would not leave
without her this time.

Even if he had to admit that he loved her. The
thought terrified him, for he knew that it would give
her an advantage over him that he was loath to hand
her. But if it was the only way he could have her, he
would be forced to own up to what he had only realized today.

He was wildly, madly, crazily in love with Emily.

Emily cast a dark look at the slimy brown creature
that huddled underneath the catmint. The rain during
the night had brought out any number of his fellow
creatures and they feasted on her plants. With a vicious
swipe of her trowel, she neatly sliced the slug in two.
That would teach the miserable things to go after her
plants.

Thank goodness the hay had been cut before the
rain. It would be a marketable product. And with the
unexpected expense of the roof repairs, she would need
every sixpence she could find.

She hoped the duke had been thoroughly irritated by her letter. Had she politely thanked him for fixing her roof, he would not have given the matter further thought. But her ungracious attack would no doubt provoke him into some sort of response. She hoped. And prayed. For she would not beg him to return. Emily only wanted him to come of his own free will. Only then could she be utterly certain of his feelings for her.

She stood, massaging her back as she thought. She had been down on her hands and knees nearly all morning tending the garden, and her back cried out at the abuse. But there was still much work to be done and she could not afford to pamper herself. She could treat herself to a warm bath in the evening as a reward.

As she moved down the row, her thoughts drifted to Jeremy. He would be home from school in less than a fortnight. She wondered if it would be difficult to keep him busy and engaged this summer after his adventure. Their simple life at Longridge would be stifling after his glimpse of the world outside. Could there be any chance of a summer at Stratton for him? Emily knelt down beside her plants again.

She heard the soft tread of footsteps on the path behind her. "You can take the full basket back to the house, Mrs. Harris," Emily said without turning around. "If you spread the herbs out very thinly over the drying racks, the dampness will evaporate quickly."

"I really think you should have someone more experienced perform such a critical task."

Emily pivoted and craned her neck to see Hart looking down at her with an amused smile upon his face. "What are you doing here?"

"It appears that I have been promoted to gardener's helper," he said.

Emily stood, acutely aware that her gown was old, damp, and dirty. She tore off her gloves, glad she had thought to wear them.

"I came to see how your new roof looks," Hart said.

He turned and looked closely at the house. "It appears to be presentable. Are the leaks gone?"

"What right did you have to order such a thing done?"

He turned back to her. "No right at all," he admitted cheerfully. "I did it simply because I wanted to."

"I did not want you to."

"I do not give a tinker's damn what you want, Emily. Regarding this matter, that is," he amended hastily. "On other matters, I might be more persuadable."

"I do not recall that there is anything of which I wished to persuade you."

"Oh?" He wrapped her hand around his arm and firmly drew her down the pathway. "You certainly did your best to persuade me that you are a woman of independent spirit."

"I am."

"See? We are in agreement already. I also recall that you insisted that you did not wish to be a dutiful wife and mother."

Emily looked at him suspiciously.

"So I have come to tell you that I am willing to concede that point. I will not expect you to be a dutiful wife and mother." He stopped and took both her hands in his. "I would only like to persuade you to be my wife. The kind of wife you would like to be."

Emily stared at him. "Pardon me for disbelieving your words, your grace, but have you perhaps suffered from some injury to the brain? You do not sound at all like the Duke of Hartford. Where is your bullying arrogance? Your domineering insistence that everything be done to your wishes?"

Hart winced. "I know I have been rather overbearing, Emily. That is why I need you. You are the only person of my acquaintance who will not allow me to ride roughshod over them. You can have the challenge of reforming me, of teaching me how to consider the wishes of others as well as my own."

"I am not a miracle worker," Emily said under her breath.

"Oh, but you are, my dear. Look what change you have wrought in only this short time. You have turned me from a confident, devil-may-care man into a mere shell of his former self."

"Why are you so determined to make me your wife?" she demanded. "Have all the women in London suddenly cocked up their toes and you are driven to desperation?"

Hart looked at her and Emily shivered at the expression in his eyes. They held neither his usual mocking smugness, nor his arrogant imperiousness. They pleaded, begged.

"I need you, Emily. I really do. I have been miserably unhappy since I left you here. No one talks back to me. No one tells me I am being an arrogant, interfering bully. I miss that. I miss you."

Emily gently drew her hands from his. "What you are missing is merely the excitement of the chase," she said, trying to deny the hope in her heart. "It was a romantic adventure, the two of us dashing across England in search of two runaway boys. I felt it too. But Hart, it was time out of time. It was not real."

"Now who is the arrogant one?" he demanded. "You are trying to tell me that what I think and feel is not real."

"But it is not," she protested. "It cannot be."

He captured her hands again. "Why not?"

Emily averted her eyes. Because she wanted it too much.

Hart took a deep breath. "I was afraid it would come to this. You are not going to relent until you have me groveling at your feet, are you?" He dropped suddenly to his knees, still keeping his hold on her hands. "Will this do, Emily? Have I repented enough?"

"Oh, Hart, do stand up. You are being ridiculous."

"You certainly know how to deflate the aspirations of a swain, my lady."

"You are no more a swain than I am the queen of England."

"I love you, Emily."

Emily turned her head and looked toward the house.

"Did you hear what I said? I said I love—"

"I heard you," she said with exasperation.

"Most women would be a bit more grateful to hear such a declaration," he said in hurt tones.

"Most women would not even look beyond the words to what lay behind," she retorted. "But I know you too well to be taken in by sweet sayings."

"You do? Now you are sounding like me again, telling me what it is I think. I love you, Emily, and the thought terrifies me. I have never loved anyone before—well, except for Phillip. And I am not at all certain I wish to be married to a woman I love. For I have the horrible feeling that she will make my life miserable."

"You do not love me," she said lightly. "You are in love with the idea of being in love."

"Oh, no, it is you," he insisted. "Why else would I be so miserable without you? Or with you, for that matter. These bricks are damn hard."

Emily laughed. "Then stop being so silly and stand up."

"But I have to convince you of my sincerity first," Hart said. "Please take pity on a poor man and say you believe me. Accept the fact that for the first and very last time in my life I am in love with a woman who is going to bully me and argue with me and force me to do all sorts of things I do not want to do, and I will not mind at all. If that is not love, I do not know what love is."

"Oh, Hart." Emily's eyes filled with tears of joy.

"Believe me, Emily. Believe me when I say I love

you with all my heart. I will allow you to dress in rags, let Jeremy's house tumble into ruins, and feed you on bread and water if it will make you feel better."

Emily tugged at his hand, trying to draw him to his feet.

"I will let you cosset and coddle both Jeremy and Phillip with your womanly ways. You can rip up the entire garden at Stratton and plant lavender and all your other herbs. Anything you wish. Anything."

"I almost think you are serious."

Hart stood, dropping her hands and placing his about her waist. "I am, Emily," he said, looking down into her eyes. "Deadly serious. I cannot live without you." He bent down and touched his lips to hers. "Come be with me. Come be with me forever. I will do anything you want, anything you ask of me." His arms tightened about her.

Emily's hands stole up to his shoulders. "I am afraid, Hart. Afraid of what loving you will bring."

He kissed her tenderly. "I will love you forever, until the last breath has left my body," he said. "Let me show you, Emily. Please let me show you."

Emily stood on tiptoe and kissed him.

"Is that a yes?" he asked.

She nodded shyly.

"Thank God," he murmured before he was lost in the joy of kissing his intended.

Some time later, when Emily had changed into a more presentable gown, they sat in the drawing room, sipping tea. She sat in the circle of his arm, her head resting on his shoulder.

"I thought you might wish a small wedding," Hart said.

"Indeed," said Emily. "With the minimum of fuss."

"Good," he said. "Is tomorrow too soon?"

She looked at him, aghast. "Tomorrow? How could we possibly be wed tomorrow?"

Hart looked at her with a sheepish expression. "I

did—ah—pay a visit to a bishop on the way here." He patted his coat. "I do happen to have a special license."

"Why, you arrogant, egotistical . . ." Emily burst out laughing. "You were so certain of me, were you?"

"No," he admitted. "I was deadly afraid. I only wanted to make certain that if I did mange to persuade you, I could get the matter taken care of before you changed your mind."

"A wise decision," she said dryly.

"If we leave this afternoon, or very early in the morning, we can be to Norfolk by late tomorrow."

"Why are we going to Norfolk?"

"You cannot expect us to be married without the two most important guests in attendance. Viscount Darrow and the Marquess of Stratton have to be there."

"Oh." Emily smiled. "And does my domineering duke have a honeymoon planned?"

"Oh, indeed," he said smugly.

"Paris?" she asked. "Rome?"

"Why, Emily, you surprise me. I thought you would easily guess the location."

"Tell me," she demanded, running her fingers lightly down his cheek.

He captured her hand and pressed a kiss on her palm. "Why, Ireland, dear lady. We are going to search for leprechauns."